My Gypsy War Diary

by Shawn D. Brink

G/H

Gabriel's Horn Publishing

Contact: editors@gabrielshornpress.com

Published by Gabriel's Horn Publishing

Publisher's Note: This novel is a work of fiction. Names, characters, places, and incidents are either products of the author's imagination or used fictitiously. All characters are fictional, and any similarity to people living or dead is purely coincidental.

Cover: Laura Vosika

First printing 2018, Minneapolis, MN

For sales, please contact editors@gabrielshornpress.com

ISBN-13: 978-1-938990-32-8
ISBN-10: 1-938990-32-3

Other Novels by Shawn D. Brink

The Space Between
The Devil's Revenge
Hell on Earth
Vengeance is Mine, a novelette

DEDICATION

I dedicate this book to the city of Norfolk Nebraska.
It was a great place to grow up.
Thanks for the memories.

ACKNOWLEDGMENTS

Above all, I thank God. For without Him, nothing is possible.

I would also like to thank Laura Vosika and her staff at Gabriel's Horn Press. My book shines because of them.

And last but not least, I would like to thank my wife and children. You are my inspiration.

CHAPTER 1 – HAUNTED MEMORIES

This is my diary. Until this moment, it has only existed in my mind, nothing but memories wrapped within my darkest depths. Now however, I find that these memories are demanding to be set free. They are screaming to be put to paper. I am not sure why they scream to me now, after all of these years. Perhaps I just need distance from it and putting ink on the page will create that distance. Or maybe, deep down, I want to relive the adventure. Regardless of the reasons, I feel compelled to write it out. I think hard on where I should even begin. It is so unbelievable after all. A primal feeling is shouting out louder than all the others. I'll start with that primal feeling—not at the beginning, but with a memory of sheer terror.

*

I stood there in that attic, holding the book that would guide me to salvation. It felt old against my fingers. In the dimness, I brought it up close to my face. The leather was cracked, but the embossed name of the book's owner still appeared brightly. No mistake, this was the artifact I had come to retrieve.

The rain pounded on the roof, reminding me of the sound of bacon frying. My stomach growled. No lie, I could have eaten some bacon right then, but the mission needed to be completed. Besides, I had no bacon.

And then—I froze in terror. Mixed with the bacon-frying, was another less distinct noise; one not created by rain, wind, or thunder. It was a rhythmic creaking.

That sound verified an unsettling fact. I was not the only one interested in the book. I was not alone in the house. Somebody was climbing the stairs.

The creeper ascended slowly, evidenced by the time that passed between each creaking reverberation. Whoever was slinking up those steps, was trying hard to slide under my radar.

Shivers squirmed up and down my spine as I looked for a place to hide. There was nowhere. The attic was an empty space, void of anything to cower behind.

For lack of options, I hurried to the blackest, furthest corner of the attic where I would be much less noticeable. But would it be enough? I crouched down into the small space where the roof slanted down to meet the floor. Cobwebs brushed my face and tickled my nose. I held my breath, fearful of a sneeze. I forced myself into a painful silence holding the old book in one hand and my flashlight in the other.

Lightning blazed through the broken attic windows and for an instant, my invisibility evaporated. Panic stabbed me, but I had committed to this hidey-hole. It was too late to move. Besides, no alternative presented itself. I hugged the book close and stared out into the darkness, praying for my salvation.

A strange light glowed upon the wall opposite from where I hid. At first, I could not understand what it was doing there or where it had come from. Then it hit me. In my terror, I had forgotten to turn off my own flashlight. I did it, just in the nick of time.

My light vanished, and a split second later, another light flickered in the stairwell.

I held my own flashlight like a bludgeoning weapon, now that it was no use for seeing in the dark. I gripped it in my hand, keenly aware of how inadequate it was compared to what I wished I had.

My body and mind were nearing the critical flash point, that moment at which panic overcomes rationality. My thoughts were of the darkness and how that darkness was my only cover—and how easily that cover could be removed with a simple swipe of the stranger's flashlight. I sank further into the valley of terror.

I struggled to remain in control of myself. I couldn't afford to lose it. I drew in a deep, calming breath. It didn't work.

As silently as possible, I slid back under the lowest part of the roof-line I could manage while still staying on my feet, trying to blend into the darkness, to make my body as small a target as possible. I squatted low, really low, ready to spring into flight at a moment's notice. There was nothing more to do but wait for the intruders to show themselves.

I didn't wait long. Behind the glare of the approaching flashlight beam, two silhouettes appeared. They didn't talk, or if they did, I couldn't hear them over the booming of my heart, the pulsing of blood through my veins, and the bacon-frying spatter of rain pounding on the roof above.

A lump formed in my throat, large and ugly. I tried to swallow it, but everything felt so dry in my mouth, as if a desert had formed in the pit of my stomach and blown a dry wind up my esophagus.

The two silhouettes emerged fully into the attic. The one with the light wielded it like Darth Vader with his light saber, murdering the darkness as he swung it slowly back and forth.

The light passed just over my head. If I had not moved back as far as I had into the shadows or crouched as low as I did, I would have, without a doubt, been caught.

"He's gone," I heard one of them say.

"How? The only way out was the stairs. We would have seen him," the second one said.

The last remnants of day had long since retreated past the western horizon, but I saw their silhouettes in front of one of the glassless attic windows as lightning flashed. The electrified light caused them to appear as black-ink devils against the whiteness of that bolt. They looked out the window, their backs to me.

What fortune they were looking away when that lightning had struck! The brilliance of that strike would have illuminated me like a flame on a candle's wick and given away the secret of my little hidey-hole.

"He could have left through this here window. Look, the roof line would allow it. Then, from the roof, it's only about a ten-foot drop."

"Well, I'll be damned," the other said with obvious frustration. "We can't very well go back and report that the stupid little imp outwitted us."

I was as frustrated as the one who was grumbling. Not only did I resent being called a 'stupid little imp', but also I had not even thought to look out the window and see if I could have made a safe escape. And now it was too late. I was trapped.

"Do you think he has it with him?" one of them asked as their flashlight beam settled upon the still open and no longer secret compartment that had hidden the book which I now held.

"What do you think?"

"Well, maybe it wasn't there to begin with?"

"Don't be such a dolt. Of course it was there. He got it and then he left. Look, you can even see the little sneak's wet footprints as he made his getaway."

Wet footprints! That last statement made the lump in my throat grow into a cancerous wad. If they saw my footprints, and if they had any brains at all, I was as good as dead. I couldn't believe I'd been so careful, and then forgotten about my wet sneakers giving me away.

I watched in horror as their flashlight beam followed my footprints. Closer and closer the light crept. Nearer and nearer it encroached to where the darkness shrouded me, inch by inch and footprint by footprint. I was going to be caught!

Just then, salvation came to me in the form of an owl. It must have been perched there in the rafters the whole time watching everything unfold. Luckily for me, it picked that moment to hoot and fly around the attic before flapping out through one of the gaping glassless windows.

The distraction was momentary, but it was all I needed. I exploded from my hidey-hole, plowing into one of them, causing their flashlight to drop to the ground.

Out the window the two of us fell, locked in some sort of weird hug, me and him, as we rolled down the roof.

Then, we were no longer rolling. We were no longer on the roof. We were falling!

So much for a soft-mud landing. Luckily, the other broke my fall with a rattling gasp.

Somehow, I managed to keep hold of the book in one hand and the flashlight in the other. I used the latter as a weapon. Two quick, hard jabs and I knew I'd broken both his face and my flashlight.

He bawled in pain. Despite the darkness, I saw, or thought I saw, blood as it streamed out of his nostrils and contrasted with his pale skin in inky miniature rivers.

I tried to get off of him, but he wrapped his arms around me. I wacked him again and felt pieces of flashlight break free in my hand.

His grip relaxed and he stopped resisting. By the way his head lulled, I judged he was unconscious. Or worse.

A gunshot rang out over the din of the storm. Mud erupted like a miniature volcano just inches from me where the bullet dug in. That got me moving.

I ran. I ran away as hard as I could. I heard more shots. I kept running.

*

You may ask yourself how I came to be in such a predicament as has just been described. Of course background is needed, some frame of reference. Now that this memory of terror is out upon the page, I can focus better. So now, let's start more appropriately at the beginning.

CHAPTER 2 - GHOSTS

My first memories of Norfolk, Nebraska were of all the ghosts. They were in every front yard like forlorn guardians of their respective houses.

I found out later that they weren't ghosts at all. We moved to Norfolk in the fall of 1978, by coincidence at the same time as the first frost of the season. Everyone had covered their rosebushes and other plants with white sheets in order to prolong their battle against the bitterness of the fast-approaching Nebraska winter.

It was a battle the residents of the town could not hope to win. They could do little more than lengthen the signs of summer, a slight extension but nothing more.

We moved to Norfolk from Clovis, New Mexico. Clovis had no rosebush-rescuing ghosts that I knew of. There really was no need for such things in Clovis. It was not a cold weather town like Norfolk.

I remember being excited to move north. It was a new place and an opportunity for new adventures.

"Dad," I asked. "When it snows, can I go sledding?"

I had never been sledding before in my life, but if TV had taught me anything, it was that sledding was the crème de la crème of childhood wintertime experiences.

My dad let out a sigh. Back then, I did not understand why this question tired him so. Now of course, I understand that such inquiries asked a thousand times by an overly excited kid can drive an adult bonkers.

I asked again, making it the thousand and first time. He nodded. I was satisfied with that answer, at least until the next time I felt the need to ask.

I always give kudos to my parents. I was a child who required extra patience on their part, and they always did their best with me even when, on occasion, I stretched their last nerves to the breaking point.

Even back then at the tender age of seven, I knew that I was different. Being different is not a bad thing necessarily, but it did sometimes require extra patience on the part of others.

Remember, this was all back in the 70s. If I was that age now, I suppose the doctors would have diagnosed me with some sort of attention deficit disorder. Back then however, such diagnoses often went undiscovered.

The year prior to moving to Norfolk was my first grade experience. I don't remember it being much fun. I tried to pay attention, honest I did; but in the end I usually zoned out, tuned out, and was left out.

As an example, if I had a dime for every time that my teacher in Clovis had asked me if I was going to eat my tie for lunch because I had forgotten to bring my Superman lunchbox along with me to the cafeteria, well I suppose I would have quite a pile of dimes today.

Yes, that is correct, I wore ties to the first grade. More precisely, I wore bolo ties.

I really don't know the reason as to why my mother insisted on this. None of the other kids' mothers made their children wear them. I guess she thought such fashion statements were suave and sophisticated.

Of course my classmates had other opinions of my tie-wearing habit and made every attempt to make sure I knew it. Two sides to every coin, I suppose.

But that was last year. That was back in Clovis. Now, I could get a fresh start and put my bolo tie wearing days behind me.

I had a positive vibe rolling around inside of me as we entered Norfolk for the very first time with all of our belongings piled into the back of a U-Haul trailer. We entered the city limits and passed a billboard stating that Norfolk was the hometown of Johnny Carson, which I thought was pretty cool. It was kind of like moving to Hollywood and not too shabby for a bolo tie-wearing kid from Clovis.

*

So we drove past the many ghostly rosebushes. We drove down First Street towards my new home, and towards an adventure that I could never have anticipated, not in a million years.

CHAPTER 3 – GYPSIES?

405 South First Street. That was our new address. My parents paid a whopping 18,000 dollars for the place, which at my young age sounded like a king's ransom. It wasn't until years later that I realized that although 18,000 dollars is nothing to flush down the toilet, it certainly was not much as far as home prices went, even by 1978 standards. It was simply what my parents could afford at the time.

Regardless, I thought the house was exceedingly awesome. It had been built back in the 1870s and virtually reeked of the past. On the top floor was an attic. The attic was cool all by itself, but what made it ultra-cool was the secret room at its far end.

In that attic, behind a fake wall, was a hidden empty space. It was only about four feet deep and twice that in width. The real-estate agent who sold my parents the house told us that back in the day, this secret room had been used to hide children from the gypsies.

Gypsies? The word sent shivers down my spine. Little did I know at the time, but in my future, that word would become a very disturbing part of my vocabulary.

"Not all gypsies were bad per se," the agent had said. "But there was *one particular* group of them that filled Norfolk's past with terror. They had a reputation of stealing anything they could get their hands on." She leaned close, her eyes wide. "That included money, livestock, and even children. Hence, the secret room."

Even at my young age, I saw the potential for myth in this story. Still, it was a cool legend and certainly added to the mystique of the place.

The house was further coolified by its electrical wiring. Being built in the 1870s, it had been constructed without electricity. Then sometime in the early 1900s, somebody had done a rather amateur retro-fit job of it.

Rather than fish wires behind the old plaster walls, the old knob and tube wiring was simply tacked up in plain view, thus part of the reason my parents got such a good price on the place. These days, such a house would never pass building code, but things were a bit more relaxed back then. Personally, I loved the weirdness of the wires. It was different and I liked different.

My room was upstairs, just down the hall from the attic. That room, I was soon to discover, was an icebox in the winter because of poor heat ventilation and a griddle in the summer because heat rises and the house had no air conditioning. Still it was my space and I liked it.

*

This was the house I moved into back in the fall of 1978. This was also the year I met our neighbor, truly a one of a kind and although she did not know it yet, a future companion on my path that would lead to the events that I described back at the beginning of this diary.

CHAPTER 4 - SKULLS

I met our new neighbor for the very first time about a week after we moved in. By then the rosebushes had all been abandoned by their ghostly protectors, the chill forcing them into cold weather dormancy.

I was playing in our driveway. It was a backyard driveway that entered into our property from the alley behind our house.

The driveway was not concrete or asphalt. For the price paid for our luxurious Norfolk living accommodations, we got a mud-rock path.

The path reminded me of pictures I had seen of old pioneer trails which in turn reminded me of old TV show westerns I liked to watch. At that time in my life, TV and me was kind of a morphed breed. My imagination had tied the two of us together into a sort of pseudo-reality knot.

The mud-rock driveway reminded me of one of my favorite TV shows *Maverick.* On that cool autumn day, at our driveway, in my imagination, I was Bret Maverick: professional card-shark/gambler and wild-west gun slinger.

Of course it was no fun to just stand there on the mud-rock and be Maverick. Things had to happen. Just like the TV character, I got into troublesome situations that often culminated in a fist-fight with some unsavory desperados.

Just like in the show, the bad guys would always get in a few good licks, just enough to make me mad and maybe knock the hat off of my head. In the end however, I always won, albeit with a few imaginary bruises.

After this particular brawl, I was extra exhausted. I swaggered over to where my hat had fallen. I picked it up, dusted it off, and returned it to my head. Then with my remaining strength, I sauntered over to the neighbor's chain link fence and leaned against it for support.

"Don't lean on my fence."

I jumped. The voice was close and unexpected. I spun, half-expecting to see one of the imaginary desperados ready for round two. Instead, I came face to face with an old woman.

I stumbled back. "I'm sorry," I said as I tipped my hat towards her in gentlemanly Bret Maverick fashion.

"I just don't want the fence to get bent up, that's all," she said as she looked me over. "Especially since you don't look like you carry enough cash to get me a new one."

Are you kidding? I thought. *Maverick always has his gambling winnings.* "Sorry ma'am," is what I actually said.

"No need for formalities," she chuckled. "You can call me Mrs. Skulls."

"Wow, what a neat name Ma'am," I said acutely aware that I was still acting quite formal due to habits of my upbringing.

"Why do you say that?" she asked. The expression on her face told me that she really did not know. "Why do you think I have a neat name?"

"Skulls," I said in total disbelief of the fact that she failed to see the total awesomeness of it. "It sounds like the name of a professional wrestler or a pirate."

A smile appeared on her face. "I suppose it does sound that way, but it is spelled differently. S–C–H–O–L–E–S," she said the letters slowly.

"Oh," I said.

"And what is your name?" she asked.

Call me Maverick, I thought to myself. Of course I did not say this out loud. Instead, I told her my name, my real name.

"Well, it's nice to meet you," she responded.

I nodded to show my feelings of mutual agreement.

"Well, I'll let you get back to… ah, whatever it was you were doing. Just try to keep off the fence, okay?"

I nodded again, but my attention deficiency problem was kicking into overdrive and I had forgotten what it was that I had actually been doing. After all, that was then and this was now. As a general rule, I lived for the now.

"What are you doing?" I asked.

"I'm spreading leaves over my vegetable garden."

"Why?"

"To add fertilizer for next spring."

I watched her do her stuff. This new neighbor was about the most interesting thing besides our new house that I had encountered since moving to Norfolk. At the time, I figured she was at least a thousand years old if she was a day. Of course, looking back on it now, my math may have been a tad off. Regardless, through my young eyes, she looked ancient.

I watched her spread the leaves and wondered if I would be capable of such labor someday when I was that old. She had a red wheelbarrow which she pushed around to disperse loads of leaves. That wheelbarrow had my attention.

"Can I help?" I asked.

Putting her hands on her hips, she stretched her back straight, let out a quiet moan, and looked at me. Those eyes possessed a twinkle that I perceived to be friendliness.

"Please?" I begged.

She rubbed her back as she said, "There's an extra set of work gloves on the back porch."

I was so excited that I had trouble finding the gate that allowed me through the fence and even more trouble locating the work gloves on the back porch, but I managed nonetheless.

I pulled on the gloves. They were old and worn and fit a little big on my child-sized hands, but I did not care because an adult other than my parents had given me an awesome job to do which put me on cloud nine.

From the back porch, I ran out and began to help. As I had suspected, it was fun work.

*

Hence a friendship was born which, over the course of the next few years, would grow into something of a giant. Little did I know then about future happenings that would test the strength of that giant. But that comes later.

CHAPTER 5 - FRIENDS

Spreading those leaves took the entire remainder of the afternoon, long enough for me to abandon my Bret Maverick persona and become just me, the kid from Clovis. It must have been about time for dinner when I helped her empty that last wheelbarrow load because my tummy was getting mighty rumbly.

I looked at Mrs. Scholes. She was kind of hunched over and leaning on a shovel that she had been using. Her free hand that was not acting as a support with the shovel was massaging her lower back.

"These old bones don't work quite like they used to," she said.

"Are you going to be okay?" I asked with genuine concern.

She chuckled. "Pretty sure. Thanks for all the help."

I smiled broadly. There was nothing I liked more than appreciation from an adult for having done a job well.

"Would you like to come inside for some cookies?"

Here is a little fact about me, I love cookies. But despite that infatuation, I shook my head, remembering one of my parent's rules. "I'm not allowed to go inside anyone's house unless my parents know where I am."

Mrs. Scholes nodded thoughtfully. "Well then, would it be okay if we sat on the back porch and ate them?"

I nodded, purposely ignoring another of my parent's rules, that being: Don't ruin your appetite with snacks before supper. Then again, this wasn't so much a snack as it was payment for services rendered.

She disappeared into her home as I sat down and removed my work gloves. They were filthy in testament to my honest day's labor.

She returned to the porch with a smile, two glasses of milk, and a plate of vanilla wafer cookies. They were store-bought, but I didn't mind. After all, I was hungry and they were technically my first paycheck.

"So," I said through a mouthful of vanilla wafery goodness. "Do you have anything tomorrow I can help with?"

"Don't talk with your mouth full. It's not polite. And don't you have school tomorrow?"

I did, but I wasn't exactly excited about it. "Yes, but I could come over after school and help you with stuff."

"Oh, I don't know. I get along pretty well all by myself. Why don't you just play with your friends after school?"

"You're the only friend I've met so far since moving here."

That statement was not entirely true. I had made a few connections at school, but there were no kids in the neighborhood that I had found. Besides, my mom had insisted on reinstating the bolo tie dress code/curse which had proven once again to be a bit of a friend inhibitor.

"Besides," I added. "At school, they teach us to always help old people."

Mrs. Scholes kind of choked a bit on her cookie. "Old? You think I am old?"

I did not in fact think she was old. I thought she was positively ancient, but her reaction made me suddenly reluctant to state those thoughts.

Mrs. Scholes must have noticed my fidgetiness. She began to laugh. "It's okay. I am pretty old, but only in years. At heart, I'm just getting started."

I smiled, happy to be let off the hook so easily.

She continued, "Being young at heart is more important than being young in years. With a young heart comes a youthful spirit."

I nodded, but in true attention deficit disorder fashion, I was already on to the next subject. "Mrs. Scholes, I noticed you have a sidewalk in front of your house."

She nodded, her face indicating that I had thrown her quite the curveball. "Um, yes. I do have a sidewalk."

"Well, when it snows, can I shovel your sidewalk for you?"

Mrs. Scholes paused for a moment, keeping me in suspense. Then, she shook her head.

"Why not?" I whined.

"My boy does that job for me already."

"You have a boy?" My hopes that other kids existed in the neighborhood suddenly escalated.

She nodded.

"Can I play with him sometime?"

"Oh, I kind of doubt it. Just because he is my boy doesn't mean he's a child. He's in his 60s and I have a feeling his playing days might be behind him."

"Oh." I said as my hopes de-escalated back to normal levels. "I was hoping there was going to be another kid in the neighborhood."

"I'm afraid not."

"Is your son like you at least? Is he young at heart?"

At that statement she laughed and slapped her knee. "I suppose he might be, but not quite like me."

I laughed along with her, although I wasn't sure what was so funny.

"My son is a quiet sort. Doesn't speak too much these days. You probably wouldn't get a lot of fun out of hanging out with him."

"Oh," I said as I did not know what else to say to that bit of information.

"How are those cookies?" she asked, suddenly changing the subject and wiping away an unexpected tear.

"Yummy," I answered. "Can I have more?"

"No sir."

"Sorry, I meant to use the magic word."

Her eyebrows raised up at this.

"Please, can I have just one more?" I folded my hands into a begging position.

This initiated another round of laughter and knee slapping from my new friend. This time, I smiled, but didn't join in. I was asking a serious question of the utmost importance after all.

"No. You'll ruin your appetite for dinner."

"Is it dinner time?" I asked, acting as if I had no idea.

She nodded.

"I'd better get home then."

"Yes, I suppose you should."

"Thanks for the cookies," I shouted as I ran through her gate and back to my side of the fence.

"Thank you for all the help," she shouted back.

*

This was my first experience with Mrs. Scholes and I knew it wouldn't be the last. I had made a new friend. It had been a good day.

CHAPTER 6 – SCOOP, TURN, DUMP

The days passed and that first autumn in Norfolk grew progressively colder. Being a boy who had only previously known Clovis' weather, I couldn't believe the temperature kept falling, yet it did, almost by the hour.

Then it happened. The first snow. I'll always remember that first snow because that was when I met Mr. Scholes.

It was one of those colder than cold mornings. In fact, as I opened my eyes and peered out from under the piles of blankets that covered me, my breath took on ectoplasmic form.

The ghosts of Norfolk had returned, albeit in a different spectral body. They no longer protected roses, but now stole my breath away and replaced it with a chill in my bones.

I got out of bed, taking most of the covers with me. Like some strange upright walking caterpillar encased in its own cocoon, I approached my window and peered out. What I saw made my jaw drop.

The drab browns and grays of dormant prairie grass and leafless trees had been replaced by the pristine white of freshly fallen snow. That blanket of whiteness covered everything, making it a whole new world.

Back in Clovis it snowed on occasion, but usually only a dusting descended upon that town and it usually melted once the desert sun rose. To my knowledge, Clovis had never been literally buried like Norfolk had on that cold day.

I ran down the stairs, skipping steps with every stride. This was a risky act, one my parents had always discouraged. My excitement level however persuaded me to throw caution to the wind.

I went straight to the radio and turned it on. Back then, there was no internet, text, or voice mail option for alerting students of snow days. It was all announced through the local radio station. I tuned into Norfolk's radio KNEN, closed my eyes, crossed my fingers, and prayed for a miracle.

I quickly realized that the DJ seemed to enjoy keeping the kids in suspense. The list of schools and other closing announcements seemed so long and the announcer seemed to speak so slowly. Then, just when I was beginning to consider reporting the radio station's torture methods to the proper authorities, the miracle happened. Glory of all glories, my school was closed.

Yes!

I asked my mother's permission to go outside and play. She said I could once I had eaten breakfast and shoveled the front walk. Well, I can tell you my oatmeal disappeared quicker than a pile of sugar on an ant hill.

Tummy full, I immediately got to work getting prepared to explore the winter wonderland that existed just outside my house. I got on my snow pants, gloves, hat, coat, boots, and scarf. Then, out the door I flew.

I left the house and entered another world, one as alien to me as the Martian landscape. I wanted nothing more than to dive in and begin the various items of play which I had reserved for this day of first snow: snow angel making, snowball manufacture, and last but not least, being the creator of my own empire of evil snowmen bent on world conquest. Before any of that however, chores were required of me.

I marched directly to the shed in our backyard and retrieved a snow shovel. Back in the front yard, on the sidewalk, I began. Scoop the snow, turn the shovel, dump the snow. It was a fairly simply process to be repeated over and over in perpetual motion until the job was done. Scoop the snow, turn the shovel, dump the snow. Scoop, turn, dump. Scoop, turn, dump and repeat. Scoop, turn, dump.

I chugged along the sidewalk like the little engine that could. *Scoop, turn, dump. Scoop, turn dump. Scoop, turn, dump. I think I can. I think I can. I think I can.*

I made pretty good time and soon a path was behind me that was relatively snow-free. I looked ahead and estimated that about half the sidewalk needed to still be done. *Scoop, turn, dump. Scoop, turn, dump. Scoop, turn, dump.* I continued onward.

At my age at the time, muscles seemed tireless and able to work indefinitely. Plus, the thought that I could play as soon as my labor was done acted like caffeine in my system and kept me hopping.

I chugged along, and like that little engine that could when he actually did, I finished my job. *I knew I could. I knew I could. I knew I could,* I said to myself as I did my last few scoops, turns, and dumps.

I straightened my back, which to my surprise seemed unwilling to straighten at first. I used my shovel for leverage and forced my way into an upright homo-sapiens type posture.

First Street was normally one of the busier streets in Norfolk, but not today. Today, it was empty except for a city-owned plow that came careening down the road with a white plume of glittery snow flying in its wake. It came. It went. It was gone, leaving me in the silence of a deserted street.

The silence was not absolute. I heard a noise. Somewhere, someone else was shoveling. *Scoop, turn, dump. Scoop, turn, dump. Scoop, turn, dump.* The shoveler was close.

I turned around. I looked for the source of the shoveling. The noise was coming from Mrs. Scholes' property. The figure who shoveled her sidewalk, I could not recognize. There were simply too many layers of clothing for identification.

The shoveler wore a pair of dark brown work overalls in addition to an old olive-green army surplus coat, gloves and hat. The army surplus coat had a hood tied tight over the shoveler's head.

"Hi," I said to the shoveler.

The shoveler turned toward me, but I couldn't see through the disguise as the figure wore a black ski mask. I did however take notice of the short stature, similar to that of my elderly neighbor, and therefore concluded this must be her boy.

I came closer. The figure resumed shoveling. *Scoop, turn, dump. Scoop, turn, dump.*

Mr. Scholes was slower than I was at this task. *Of course he would be*, I thought to myself. He was old, and Mrs. Scholes told me he was not even as young at heart.

"If you want, I can help you, then we can get done quicker," I offered to Mr. Scholes.

The sound of shoveling ceased. The figure turned toward me, but said nothing. He just stared.

"It's okay Mr. Scholes," I said, feeling a bit awkward. "I know your mom. She's a real nice lady. We're pretty good friends."

Mr. Scholes just continued to stare. He made no movement. He said nothing.

I remembered Mrs. Scholes telling me her boy was the quiet type, not a talker. Now, I understood what she meant and it made me a bit uneasy, but I had committed by this point, so I pushed as hard as I dared.

"Please let me help?"

After a moment that seemed an eternity, the figure nodded a slow nod. Well, that was all the permission I needed.

"Thanks Mr. Scholes. You won't regret this. I'm a real hard worker."

With those words, my shovel went back into action. *Scoop, turn, dump. Scoop, turn, dump. Scoop, turn, dump.*

Out of the corner of my eye, I could see Mr. Scholes. At first, he just stood there staring at me through the eye-sockets of that mask. After a moment, he shrugged and then joined in.

Together we scooped. Together we turned. Together, we dumped. We repeated this process until Mrs. Scholes' sidewalk was clear.

CHAPTER 7 – A MYSTERY

My first winter in Norfolk had been quite an experience. The native Norfolkians (as people from Norfolk like to be called) confirmed it was a doozy of a winter even by their standards. The snow just kept falling, plain and simple.

The excitement I had with the first snow was a bit less with the second and still less with the third. By February, I believe I had what native Norfolkians refer to as the Nebraska winter blues which basically meant that I thought winter stunk on ice (no pun intended).

I did what I could to occupy myself during the darkness of winter. Sometimes, I daydreamed about spring, but mostly I spent the days annoying my parents with the incessant symptoms of my cabin fever.

In my parent's defense, they did what they could for me. My dad, true to his promise, took me sledding numerous times. That was a rush, but like riding a roller coaster over and over, the rush became less with every repetition until it bordered on the mundane.

A lot of my time was spent at school or at home doing homework. I discovered something at school that year. I discovered a fact that I had actually suspected for a while, that being that I was not the sharpest pencil in the box, at least not by academic standards. I was on the passing side of things, but only marginally; *stupid attention deficit disorder.*

I realized that year that God had not created me to sit at a desk. I was a hands-on kind of guy. That was why I enjoyed things like shoveling snow in the winter and spreading leaves over gardens in the fall.

That winter, I wondered about Mrs. Scholes, I had not seen her for a while. My mom said she was fine, but at her age, most people choose to stay inside during the winter months. I understood, but Mrs. Scholes was really my only friend in the neighborhood, so it still kind of a bummer.

Anyway, even though the snow had lost its luster, I still enjoyed shoveling. Scoop, turn, dump. Scoop, turn, dump; what was there not to like really? It was repetitive. It was physical and did not require much attention to keep doing it. It was my kind of job.

Whenever it would snow, I would always try to get both ours and Mrs. Scholes' walk shoveled before her boy got there, but in this regard, I consistently failed.

Mr. Scholes was always on the scene by the time I got out to start. He was always dressed in the same overalls, army surplus coat, gloves, hood, and ski mask.

I always looked for his car, but never noticed one parked in Mrs. Scholes' driveway or back behind in the alley. I asked him once if he lived close by. He nodded. I asked if he just walked here to shovel. Again, he nodded. I liked Mr. Scholes, but he was not a great conversationalist and that was a fact.

He always let me help shovel, and that was a nice thing because as I already had mentioned, I liked that kind of work. One thing confused me though. The man lived nearby and always walked to his mom's house to shovel her walk, yet there were never any footprints in the snow showing which direction he had come from.

A mystery.

CHAPTER 8 – A MISSION

The winter held on tight, so tight in fact that I became convinced it would never leave. This was ludicrous thinking of course.

Even so, the snow didn't completely melt until mid-April. Although once melted, things began to really warm up. By the end of April, green things were beginning to grow, and by mid-May, the flowers were in full bloom.

It was at this time, on a warm Sunday morning, that I saw the first signs of life from my neighbor's house. Mrs. Scholes emerged from her home like some animal coming out from a deep winter's hibernation. At first, she only stuck her head out through the barely-open screen door. Then, as cautious as a mouse who feared the unseen danger of a bird of prey, the rest of her emerged from hiding.

"Good morning!" I shouted with enthusiasm.

She must not have seen me because she flinched at the sound of my voice, nearly skittering back into her home. Wide eyed and nervous, her eyes peaked out through the screen door, searching for what startled her, but when she found me, her face lit up.

"Good morning!" she said with enthusiasm equal to that which I had dealt out to her.

"Did your boy tell you how much I helped him this last winter?"

Her grin widened. "Why yes. Yes he did."

"He didn't mind me helping I hope."

"On the contrary, he said his back was not as sore this year as in the past because of you. I do believe he appreciated your help very much."

"Good. He never said a word to me and I wanted to make sure he wanted me helping."

"He's one of the strong silent types," she said. "He's been like that for as long as I care to remember."

I nodded.

"Well, what are your plans for today?" she inquired.

I was shocked. My plans were the same every Sunday morning, and at that age, I assumed everyone's Sunday plans mimicked mine. So I was a little taken aback that she even asked. "I'm going to Church and Sunday School."

"I see," she said. "Will this be taking up your entire day?"

"We get done around lunch time."

She nodded.

"Why?" I asked.

"Well, I was planning to walk down to the grocery store for supplies this afternoon and wondered if you wanted to tag along?"

"It would have to be after I am done with lunch," I said thinking about the level of sanctity that my parents always put on Sunday's main meal.

"That's fine, the store doesn't open until noon on Sundays anyway. Just come over when lunch is done."

I looked at Mrs. Scholes. It suddenly struck me that she was in her pajamas while I was dressed in my Sunday best. My parents had always told me that God didn't care how you dressed to church as long as you came (although for some reason, I was always expected to wear slacks, a dress shirt, and the ever-present bolo tie). Regardless, Mrs. Scholes was just a little too casual in my opinion.

"What church do you go to Mrs. Scholes?"

"I don't," she said flatly.

I was shocked. Mrs. Scholes was old. Who knew how much time she had before meeting her maker. "Do you want to come with us? There's plenty of room in the car and I know my dad wouldn't mind a bit if you tagged along."

The smile left her face. "Thanks, but no."

"Ah come on. Why not?"

"It's been a long time since I set foot in a church," she answered.

"That's okay. My dad says it doesn't matter if it's been a while as long as you come back."

I couldn't recall my dad ever actually saying those exact words, but it always helped a kid's argument if you said that an adult endorsed your point of view. Plus, I had a feeling my dad would have said that, or something like that if he had been asked, so I didn't consider it a lie per se.

She shook her head. "Just come over after lunch."

I noticed her voice had changed through the course of that conversation. By the end, it had a gruff quality to it. Regardless, with persistence being one of my best qualities, I would have continued asking her from different angles, but there was no one to ask. She had retreated back into her house like a mouse who had spotted the bird of prey and fled into safer realms.

Poor Mrs. Scholes, I thought as I got into the back seat of my parent's Chevy Vega. I had never dreamed somebody of her age would not want to go to church. For goodness sake on any given Sunday morning, it seemed nearly the whole congregation was her age. It had been that way in Clovis and it was no different in Norfolk. I thought it was just something old people did.

As the Vega rumbled down First Street and towards the church, I realized something. Mrs. Scholes was my friend, and as her friend, it was my duty to help her.

Right then and there, in the back seat of the car, I made a promise to God that come Hell or high water I was going to get Mrs. Scholes back into the fold. It would be my mission.

I mulled my new mission over and over in my mind. I wasn't sure how I was going to do it, but somehow I would.

CHAPTER 9 - LUTHERANS

We were Missouri Synod Lutherans. That denomination's services, back in the late 70s was not known for their entertainment value. This held especially true for children and super especially true for children who already had problems paying attention, ergo me.

The only music was from an old pipe organ. The only organist was, from my perspective about 350 years old. The only hymns the ancient organist seemed to know were those composed back in the sixteenth century by Martin Luther himself.

On that particular Sunday morning, I had an especially hard time focusing. In addition to all the normal difficulties, I had other things weighing heavily on my mind. I tried to pay attention to the sermon, cross my heart and hope to die. I tried to tell myself it was more important than anything else at that moment, but so very much was going on in my head and vying for my attention.

The preacher spoke God's word and I am sorry to say none of it soaked in. Then the sacrament of Holy Communion was given.

Children in the Missouri Synod Lutheran denomination cannot participate in communion until they're confirmed. I had not yet been confirmed and so remained in my seat while the ushers directed the post-confirmed majority to the front to be given Christ's body and blood.

I was excited about communion. Even though I couldn't partake, I knew it meant the service was almost over.

Communion was completed. The doxology was given. We were dismissed!

Of course dismissal did not mean a free for all mad rush for the door. No way Jose. Missouri Synod Lutherans are an orderly bunch.

There was a system. The ushers nodded to each row of pews, thus giving that row permission to exit. We filed out when allowed and shook the pastor's hand when it was our turn, giving the obligatory congratulations on a sermon well executed.

At this point, I could see the door marked with the glowing electric exit sign above it. That glowing sign beckoned me.

We were so close to getting out of the joint. I bit my lip to contain my excitement. It didn't work. It only gave me a sore lip.

Thoughts of rebelling against the Lutheran system of order bombarded my mind. I wanted nothing more than to push through the crowd dragging my parents behind me, forcing them through that wonderful door.

I committed this atrocity repeatedly, but only in my mind. If I had actually perpetrated such an uncivilized act, I would have likely ended up in the Pastor's study for a complete evaluation in order to make sure I was true Lutheran material and relatively devil-free.

Finally, we escaped. *What was wrong with the Vega?* I thought repeatedly as we drove home. It seemed to be moving even more sluggishly than usual.

Through my dad's past griping, I had learned that the Vega, although heralded as the latest and greatest by Chevrolet, turned out to be a bit of a lemon, and that was putting it nicely.

In retrospect however, the sluggishness of the vehicle that day was probably due to my state of mind. I stared from the back seat at the speedometer. This was an easy task for me given the fact that no seatbelt law restricted my movements back then.

We were going exactly 30 miles per hour. That was the speed limit on First Street and a rule my dad had never violated. The limit could have been a hundred miles an hour and it would not have been fast enough for me that day.

Once home, I did my best to make up for lost time. I ran up to my room and virtually ripped off my church clothes, letting them fall where they chose. I think my bolo tie may have landed under my bed, a complete coincidence of course, not that it mattered because the required tie was not mandatory on non-school days except for at church.

I put on my non-church/non-school clothes—a pair of boot-cut jeans that I liked because I thought it made me look tough. Also, I put on a Duke's of Hazard T-shirt and black cowboy boots. After all, what is the point of boot-cut jeans if you don't wear your boots?

Over the whole ensemble, I pulled on a red Nebraska Cornhusker hooded sweatshirt. It was still jacket weather in Norfolk and layers were still the norm.

Back down the stairs I flew and took my seat at our dining room table. Most everything had been set. My mother's meatloaf was the centerpiece along with meatloaf's good old pals, mashed potatoes, gravy, and green beans.

Normally, I was expected to help get things ready, but I had asked my parent's permission to go with Mrs. Scholes right after lunch to the grocery store and so they had let my duties slide so that I could get ready quicker.

I wanted to simply devour the contents of my plate and scoot, but I knew doing so before my dad said pre-meal prayer would be a huge mistake if not sacrilegious. Not only did I believe God deserved thanks for the 'bounty set before us,' but I didn't want to incite the wrath of my parents who firmly believed that saying pre-eating prayers was simply doing God's will.

I sat there like a trained dog with a treat balanced on its nose until I heard the command word *amen.* Then, I dug in.

I was just one step short of being Ralph's little brother from the movie *A Christmas Story* as I devoured my potatoes and meatloaf. I tried to hide my green beans, but my mother caught me. I had to eat five. I did it quickly because number one, I liked green beans about as much as I liked school, and two I wanted to bolt out of there as soon as I could.

Once that fifth bean had disappeared down my throat, I was dismissed. I left without even asking about dessert which was against my character. I did it nonetheless.

Out the door I went, across the lawn to Mrs. Scholes' gate. I didn't have to knock. She opened the door just as I was bounding onto her front porch.

"I've been waiting for you. Are you ready?"

I nodded.

She pulled a strange looking cart out of her home and then locked her door.

I had never seen a cart like that. It was made of the same metal tubing and wire as was your average everyday shopping cart, but it only had two wheels. It reminded me of the dolly my dad's buddy had brought over to help us load the U-Haul back in New Mexico, but unlike that dolly, this one had a deep wire basket attached to it.

"What is that?" I asked indicating the cart.

"I haven't driven since 1965. I need something to haul my groceries in. It's either this, or I'll have to try and balance all the groceries on my head."

I snickered at that mental picture. She snickered back.

"So we're walking?" I asked.

Mrs. Scholes nodded.

"How far is it?"

"Oh," Mrs. Scholes said as she rubbed her chin. "Three or four blocks give or take."

I thought this distance over. I knew I could do it, but I wondered about my poor old neighbor. "Can you walk that far?"

She began to laugh. "Yes. I've been doing it since 1965. I think I'll manage today even with you slowing me down."

"Why can't you drive?" I asked.

"It's my eyes. They don't work like they used to. I can't pass the driver's test."

"Not even with glasses?"

She shook her head. "They don't make glasses strong enough for me, dear."

I thought about this and, in true 'me' fashion, blurted out what came to mind. "Why doesn't your boy drive you?"

"Why are you so full of questions?"

I grinned awkwardly. "I'm a kid I guess."

She laughed. "You guess?"

I nodded, happy that my remark brought a laugh even though I wasn't sure why it had. I was just relaying a fact after all.

"I guess you are a kid," she said with a chuckle. "I guess you are."

*

At my age at the time, I was not a good judge of distance. I had no idea how far three blocks was. It turned out not to be very far at all.

I could have done it in half the time using my young muscles to their fullest. It took a bit longer with Mrs. Scholes in tow. I didn't mind. She was my friend.

We walked. We talked. She seemed happy to have a companion on the trip, which made me feel all warm and fuzzy inside. She even let me pull the cart for her, which was a nice thing for her to allow, because I liked being useful to others.

The cart was easy to pull to the grocery store. The way home however, was a different story. Mrs. Scholes had packed it to the brim with her provisions, weighing it down considerably. But a job was a job. I pulled it just the same.

Mrs. Scholes seemed appreciative of my efforts. In fact, she paid me with a chocolate bar for my trouble. *Wow, my second paycheck,* I thought. First cookies, and now chocolate bars. I noticed a pattern. I guess she'd figured out food was a good motivator for the likes of me.

As I pulled the grocery-laden cart, I began to think of the events from that morning. It bothered me that Mrs. Scholes didn't attend a church. It was then I remembered my self-imposed mission.

"Mrs. Scholes," I said as nonchalantly as I was able.

"What?"

"What are you doing next Sunday morning?"

"I can't tell you that"

"Oh," I said. This response stumped me momentarily. "Why not?"

"Why not?" she said with mild surprise. "Well, for one thing, I can't say because next Sunday is a whole seven days from now and at my age, I don't plan that far ahead."

At this answer, I grinned. I didn't grin too much. I didn't want her to know that I had her just where I wanted her. I was just about to give her my sales pitch about coming to church with me next week. I opened my mouth to speak.

"I know what I am not going to do," she added before I could get out my spiel.

"What's that?"

"I am not going to go to church and that is final." And her voice conveyed that finality.

My grin evaporated. "Ah, come on."

She remained silent so I pressed her. "Aren't we friends?"

"Of course we're friends."

"Well, my pastor says that friends don't keep friends out of heaven."

She laughed and not in her normal good-natured way. "Trust me, kid. Heaven doesn't want me and neither does your Jesus."

"He does," I said with conviction. "Jesus loves everyone."

"And you believe that?"

"The Bible says it, and you've got to believe the Bible."

She shook her head. "I don't think God has a place for someone like me."

"Sure he does. Just come to church with me and you'll see."

"I said *no!*"

Considering she had just said we were friends, her voice at this point didn't sound very friendly. My pastor says Christians should be bold for Christ, so I pressed a bit further. "Why not?"

"Why not? You want to know why not?"

I wasn't sure I did, but I nodded anyway.

"I'll tell you. It's because of the damned gypsies."

"The gypsies?" A chill ran down my spine as I recalled the secret room in our attic.

"Yes. Now let's change the subject, please."

"But…" I began.

"Why don't you take your pay right now," she said as she unwrapped my chocolate bar for me and inserted it into my gaping mouth.

She knew me pretty well. Chocolate was one thing that could get me to shut up.

I ate my pay. It was good. Still, dark thoughts of gypsies danced in my head.

CHAPTER 10 - JAKE

I didn't see Mrs. Scholes again for almost a week. I had heard that sometimes pushing Jesus onto people too hard can push them away. I sincerely hoped this was not why Mrs. Scholes was avoiding me. She was my only real friend after all.

I got up the next Saturday and could safely say spring had sprung. I didn't lament winter's death, not one bit.

I threw on my favorite Dukes of Hazard T-shirt, a pair of non-boot-cut jeans and my Chuck Taylor sneakers. I left off my Cornhusker sweatshirt and ran out the back door. I took a deep breath of the sweet, warm air.

With a glimmer in my eye, I promptly chased all the rabbits and squirrels out of my yard, which was something I did at that age. To this day, I don't know if that was normal behavior, but it was what I did nonetheless.

This proved to be a more difficult task than I had first thought. At that time of year, the critters were more interested in each other than me. Besides, if I chased the rabbits away, the squirrels would simply come down out of their trees. If I chased the squirrels back up, the rabbits returned. It was a never ending battle, but one I didn't mind fighting.

My frenzied chase was interrupted. "My land!" Mrs. Scholes' voice boomed. "What on Earth are you trying to do?"

I called off the pursuit and looked over at her. She was staring at me from her back porch. Her hands were fisted and on her hips, but her smile gave away that she wasn't serious about her admonishing look.

"I don't know," was my reply. It was a reply I gave quite commonly; probably too often.

"Well, you're tiring me out just watching you."

I grinned, happy in the knowledge she didn't seem to be trying to avoid me after all. "Well, I'm not tired out, not one little bit." I began running laps around the yard just to prove it.

She laughed. "I guess that's one of the many blessings of youth, endless energy."

I continued doing my laps.

"Enjoy it now," she called. "It's a fleeting blessing."

At this I stopped. "What?" I didn't know what *fleeting* meant.

"What do you mean *what*?"

"What's fleeting mean?"

She laughed again. "It means someday you'll end up like me, and that day will arrive quicker than you think."

"Never!" I replied with conviction.

"Trust me. One day you'll wake up and wonder where all that energy went."

I shook my head resolutely which caused another eruption of laughter from her.

"Before you realize it," she said.

"Nope. I'll be like Peter Pan, young forever."

Mrs. Scholes' laughter died down as she wiped her eyes which always seemed to water when she found me humorous. "So Mr. Pan, what are your plans for today?"

"I don't know," came again my most popular of replies.

One of the perpetual problems with us kids at that time was the fact we had too much free time and not enough things to do in order to fill it. We had no jobs. We had no responsibilities. That was one of the perks of being a kid.

"It's Saturday," she said matter-of-factly.

"I know."

"So are you just going to chase squirrels and rabbits all day long?"

I smiled. "Maybe."

"Well, I saw Bob Zesto's just opened for the summer. What would you say to an ice cream cone there?"

"I don't know," I said yet again.

"Why do you always say that?"

"It's just that I don't know what I would say to an ice cream cone. They don't have ears after all so they wouldn't be able to hear me no matter what I said to it."

Mrs. Scholes smiled. "Are you telling a joke?"

I smiled. I was.

"Come with me to Bob Zesto's. I'll buy you a cone, my treat."

On thinking about her offer, I decided I needed further clarification. "Mrs. Scholes?"

"Yes?"

"That sure is nice of you, but can I get some ice cream in the cone?"

Well, Mrs. Scholes slapped her knee and had a laughing fit right then and there. I had learned that when adults did that, you usually got what you asked for, so I excused myself to go ask permission from my mom. When I came back, Mrs. Scholes was still giggling slightly.

"I can come," I said.

"Great," she said as she wiped a laughter-tear from her eye. "Just wait a moment while I go inside and get my purse."

That said, she went back into the house and I went back to chasing the squirrels and rabbits. Just then, the rabbits all ran away and the squirrels stopped chattering at me from their perches in the trees. Everything suddenly grew very still.

I stood there wondering what had changed. Then I heard, through the stillness a menacing sound. It was a low, rumbling noise. I wasn't sure why, but that sound put ice in my veins.

I turned toward this new noise and came face to face with Jake. Jake was one of our neighbor's dogs, a giant schnauzer.

I didn't really like Jake much. He roamed pretty much wherever he pleased and considered the entire neighborhood his territory. He wasn't vicious, just kind of a pain in the neck.

"Hey Jake," I said as I put out my hand so he could sniff me. "Be a good boy."

I was actually glad to see Jake at that moment. I'd seen posters of him around the neighborhood. Apparently, he'd been missing for a while. I guess he'd found his way home.

Jake was acting weird even for him. I retracted my hand. Something about that dog seemed off. His fur was mangy. His eyes had a strange look about them, and his mouth was covered with froth. It looked as if he'd just chugged a beer and forgot to wipe away the foam.

The idea of Jake sitting in a bar chugging beer put me at ease. I laughed at my own silly thought.

"Stay still."

The voice I heard had a deadly serious tone to it. I looked up from the growling Jake. Mrs. Scholes was on her porch. Her purse was on the ground next to her, open and partially spilled out as if she had accidentally dropped it.

She didn't look like herself. Her face was as pale as the recently melted Nebraska snow. She also had a strange look in her eyes, but unlike Jake's, hers appeared to be fear.

"Don't move." Her voice was not overly loud, but wound tighter than a banjo string.

"It's just Jake, Mrs. Scholes," I said trying to relieve her fears.

I began to reach out my hand to pet Jake. I thought this would convince her the dog was friendly.

"Stop!" Mrs. Scholes hissed.

I did stop. I looked carefully at Jake. He didn't look right. Maybe he was sick.

I examined him from where I stood. His coat was nasty. And those eyes, there was something about them that unsettled me. They didn't seem to look at me as much as look through me somehow. Furthermore, that beer foam didn't go away from his beard. Instead, it seemed to be growing.

I watched the foam drip to the ground. *That could not be normal*, I thought. *Definitely, Jake was sick.*

"What's wrong with him?" I asked.

"Rabies," was the one word reply from Mrs. Scholes.

That single word made my heart beat faster. I had seen *Old Yeller*. I knew what rabies was, or at least I knew enough to understand why Mrs. Scholes was so afraid.

The realization of my predicament suddenly hit me. I took a cautious step back from Jake, and Jake took one towards me at the same time.

I know it is not a manly thing to admit, but I began to cry a little. Five minutes ago, I was getting ready to eat a Bob Zesto's cone with the ice cream included and everything. I had not prepared myself for the possibility that I would die that day and definitely had not prepared myself for the possibility I would die by means of a rabid-dog mauling.

"Stay calm," Mrs. Scholes' voice trailed to me. Her voice sounded so much more distant all of a sudden.

"Good boy," I sobbed to Jake.

Jake did not look like a good boy. He looked like a Devil-dog straight out of Hell. His entire emaciated body seemed to vibrate with the constant low growling emanating from him.

I was standing downwind from the Devil-dog. I caught a whiff. His odor was horrid. It made me want to gag.

Out of the corner of my eye, I could see a vague figure that I assumed was Mrs. Scholes. The figure was descending the porch steps, holding something.

I turned towards the figure, hoping Mrs. Scholes was brandishing a loaded elephant gun or better yet a fully automatic AK-47. At the very least I hoped for a syringe full of rabies vaccine. I was greatly disappointed.

She held a broom. That was all, just a broom. What was she going to do, sweep Jake away from me?

"No. Go back," I said to her. Her bravery had been noted, but so had her choice of weaponry.

I doubt if she heard my command. Fear had robbed me of my voice. It only came out as a whisper.

Jake lulled his Devil-dog head from side to side. The growl deepened. The mad look in his eyes called out to me. *I'm going to tear you apart,* they said without words.

"I've been working on the railroad, all the live long day," Mrs. Scholes' suddenly began a familiar tune.

I looked at her, puzzled. So did Jake. If this had been any other situation, I might have laughed at the spontaneous singing, but this was not another situation. This was straight-up life or death, no joke.

To this day, I don't know why she started singing. All I know is that people are prone to do weird things when stressed. I suspected she was beyond stressed. She was likely more along the lines of bat-guano-crazy terrified. I know I was.

Regardless of her rational, she continued her song, this time with revised lyrics. "*I have never been so scared, not since D-day.*"

Jake fully turned his body toward the hero with the broom. The hero continued to sing.

"*I am going to hit this dog, then I want you to run. Run and don't turn back, unless you have a gun.*"

Slowly she raised the broom and my heart went cold. A slight breeze was blowing, wiggling her ancient-lady muscles and revealing her for what she was; nothing more than a frail, elderly woman. I knew she didn't stand a chance, but didn't know what I could do to stop what was about to go down.

Jake prepared to pounce. I continued to do nothing. The broom came down with all of the hero's might.

I suddenly thought what I could do. I kicked at Jake. The target was his groin.

I missed, lost my balance and landed flat on my butt. This was not going to end well.

As I fell, I heard a loud popping noise. Confusion ensued.

Through my tears, I could see Mrs. Scholes. She looked as if she were about to hyperventilate.

At her feet was Jake. Jake was dead.

CHAPTER 11 – GUARDIAN ANGELS

Mrs. Scholes spoke with the Norfolk police. She felt it was very important the proper authorities know about a rabid dog attack. I heard her say to them, "Where there's one rabid animal there's bound to be more."

Who shot Jake? That was the burning question in my mind. I was pretty sure Mrs. Scholes' broom had not been loaded, so where did the bullet come from? I really wanted to know, but being just a kid, I knew it wasn't my place to ask questions at such adult moments. I dared not ask it.

The police did not say it out loud, but I suspected they were stumped as well. The bullet had sliced right through Jake's body and just kept going. They hadn't yet found the slug nor had they determined which direction the bullet had hit him from.

The cops searched diligently for the spent casing, but again they came up empty handed. I myself understood why. I had watched enough TV to know if you were a sniper worth your salt, you always pick up your empty shells and took them with you when you left the scene of the crime.

I heard the police tell Mrs. Scholes they weren't going to drop the investigation. Discharging a firearm within city limits is serious business after all. Personally, I was kind of glad somebody had broken that law. That mystery shooter had saved my life.

Mrs. Scholes told the police that crucial fact, and they promised they were not going to arrest whoever had been responsible. They simply wanted to make sure he or she knew such action should be reserved only for extreme defense situations.

Again, I thought to myself—the guy saved my life. In my mind they should not even talk to this guy if they find him except maybe to give him some kind of award for bravery and give him one of those over-sized keys to the city or let him ride in the Lavitsef Day parade. ('Lavitsef' is 'Festival' spelled backwards and the Lavitsef Day parade was an annual Norfolk tradition).

The rendering plant truck came and hauled away the remains of

Jake the Devil dog. The guys who took him wore special suits, gloves, and masks. Then they put some sort of chemical on the lawn where Jake's body had been and told me to stay away from that spot for at least twenty-four hours.

The police asked me again and again if I had touched Jake. I didn't think I had. Finally, the last officer departed and I was left feeling exhausted and still without an ice cream from Bob Zesto's. Not that I particularly wanted one anymore.

I turned to Mrs. Scholes. She looked paler than usual. I had to ask her the million dollar question. "Who shot Jake?"

"I don't know," she replied.

Something in her voice made me suspicious. I narrowed my eyes, put my hands on my hips, and tapped one of my feet up and down. I had once seen an episode of *The Brady Bunch* where Mrs. Brady did that action and it seemed to coax the truth out of Marsha Brady when Marsha was clearly hiding something.

Apparently however, such actions only work on TV shows or Brady Bunch family members. Mrs. Scholes remained silent. I continued my actions nonetheless.

"Stop doing that!" she snapped at me after a minute or so. "I said I don't know who shot Jake and that's the honest to goodness truth."

I nodded knowing that when somebody says 'honest to goodness,' usually they're being less than honest and sometimes less than good.

"But," she continued, "I can tell you this isn't the first time something like this has happened."

"Somebody has been shooting more dogs?" I was shocked.

She rolled her eyes. "No. You take things too literally."

"Oh." I didn't know what the word 'literally' meant, but I was sure she was probably right, maybe. Either way, I felt a bit sheepish and dealt with it by staring down at my Chuck Taylors.

"I mean I have been unexplainably protected before."

I looked up. "You have?"

She nodded. "I'm not one to believe in that church stuff, but if I was, I would say I had a guardian angel."

"Wow, a guardian angel that shoots guns!" I pictured GI Joe with wings, a halo, and a harp that doubled as some sort of hard core military weapon.

She laughed. "Maybe that's the kind of angels that guard the unchurched."

I thought about this. "How many times has this happened before?"

"Plenty."

"When?" I was astounded.

Mrs. Scholes' stare traveled from me to what I assumed was a distant memory from her past. "I don't recollect that I've ever told you why I don't drive these days."

"Sure you did. You told me your eyes were too bad to pass the exam."

She frowned at that statement. I was still at that innocent age where I was learning things to say versus things better left unsaid. I mentally filed that statement under the later for future reference.

"It was because a while back, I got into a car accident."

"A wreck?"

She nodded.

"Was it a bad one?"

"It was bad enough."

"Was it your fault?"

She nodded again. "When you hit a tree, it's hard to convince yourself it's the tree's fault for being planted where your car went careening off the road."

I smiled a little at that mental picture. In the cartoons I liked to watch, trees uprooted themselves and jumped into the path of cars all the time, but she was right; I had never witnessed such a thing in real life.

"I was telling the truth when I said my eyes were too bad to pass the exam, but that wreck was my wake-up call."

"Oh," I said.

"Anyway, I was hurt and couldn't get myself out of the car. That's when the flames started shooting from under my hood. I could feel the heat coming through the dash. If the gas line had ignited, I'd have been a goner," she said as her eyes grew wide.

"So, how did you get out?" I asked, completely enthralled with the story.

"Suddenly, these arms grabbed me. The first thing I noticed about them was they were strong. Those arms pulled me from the car. The next thing I knew, I was being hauled away from the wreck, firemen-carry style. Then there was an explosion.

"Was it the car? Did the gas line ignite?" I yelled, unable to control my excitement.

She nodded, "It was the car, but I didn't make that realization instantly. All I knew at that moment was that my ears were ringing, and exceedingly warm. I found out later that the warmth came from the blood oozing from them. A wall of intense heat blew past. In addition, I felt dizzy. A blast like that can be quite disorienting let me tell you."

"Oh my gosh," was all I could think to say at that point.

"If I'd been there in that driver's seat just a few more seconds, I'd have been nothing more than bits and pieces."

"Who pulled you out?"

She shrugged. "There were lots of witnesses, but the ones who saw him said that they didn't recognize him. He saved me and then just faded away into the crowd.

"And you never got a good look at him?"

"All I saw were his arms. And also his backside as he carried me, but that was all."

"Weird," I exclaimed.

"Very weird," she agreed.

"So, you have a guardian angel."

"I guess so."

"And knowing this, you still won't go to church?" I was exasperated with that fact.

"Don't start honey."

I wanted to say more, but the sudden, bitter look in her eyes made me close my mouth. There would be other opportunities, but now was not the time.

CHAPTER 12 - DEPRESSION

For the next four years, my friendship with Mrs. Scholes grew. This was a good thing. For I did not know it yet, but unbelievable events were on the horizon, just around the corner in fact. These unbelievable events would test the strength of our bond. If I were a gypsy fortune-teller, then maybe I would have known what was coming. Maybe I could have prepared somehow. No such revelation revealed itself to me. I was no fortune-teller and I had no gypsy blood. This was probably for the best. The events to which I allude to are terrifying. If I had known about them before-hand it would have only piled on the anxiety.

*

Those pre-catastrophe days were alright. Mrs. Scholes helped me with my school work. In exchange, I helped her with grocery shopping and gardening, and shoveled snow with her boy in the winter.

To my chagrin and despite my best efforts, I was never able to get her to come to church. This bothered me because I felt Jesus was somebody she really needed in her life. I vowed to myself and to God not to give up on that goal.

Besides the whole church thing, I tried a few more times to get her to talk about the gypsies, or why she had protection from guardian angels; but she was tight lipped. After four years I nearly gave up learning about those subjects.

Then, in 1982, Norfolk hit on hard times. Lots of new people moved to town that had not been there before, and they all seemed to be looking for work. The problem was, the town already had enough people to fill most of the jobs. There just wasn't a lot of wiggle room there.

I asked Mrs. Scholes one day where all the new people had come from and why they did not have jobs.

"They came from the same place I did," Mrs. Scholes answered.

By this time, we had been friends long enough I didn't need to ask for further explanation. The quizzical look I gave her was enough to entice further details.

She sighed. "Lots of people around here are losing their farms."

"How do you lose a farm?" I asked. "It's a big thing and never goes anywhere."

I was eleven and not that naïve, but I thought it was a pretty funny joke. Mrs. Scholes did not laugh.

"This is serious," she said. "The banks are taking farms away from the farmers."

"Why?" I wanted to know.

"Because the banks loaned the farmers money, but with the harvests the way they've been these last few years, a lot of them couldn't pay the banks back. So, they got foreclosed on."

I was appalled. "Why would banks loan money to farmers if the farmers wouldn't be able to pay them back? And why would they take the farm? How can the farmers get a harvest and pay the banks back without the farm to grow the crops?" And with that, I ran out of both breath and questions.

She smiled a sad smile. "Life's not always fair."

"Well, it shouldn't be that way," I blurted.

She nodded in agreement. "Last year, it was dry and hot and the crops scorched. The year before that, it did nothing but rain and the fields flooded."

I thought back. I remembered the drought and how everything that year looked more like how I remembered New Mexico, than the Nebraska I had come to know and love. I also remembered the summer of floods. Norfolk had been a safe place that year. We had levies and pumps to keep things relatively dry.

However, outside city limits was a different story. I remembered seeing pictures on the news of farmers in boats with pitchforks. They were spearing for carp. The only strange thing was that they weren't on a lake or river, but floating over their submerged soybean and corn fields.

I could still remember one witty newspaper headline from that year. *No Crops, Just Crappies.* I believe that was from the pages of *The Norfolk Daily News.*

I recalled Mrs. Scholes saying the people came from the same place she did. "So this happened to you?"

Mrs. Scholes nodded.

"I always thought you were just born at your home on First Street."

Mrs. Scholes laughed. "I've been here on First Street for a long time kiddo, I'll grant you that, but not my whole life. I used to live on a farm not too far from here."

"And you lost it?"

"We lost it in 1935. I loved that place. I still miss it."

"Did the bank take it?" I asked using my newly acquired knowledge. She nodded.

"What a bunch of jerks," I said with disgust.

"Now don't blame them," she sighed. "It was the Great Depression after all."

"Oh yeah?" I said.

"Do you know about the Great Depression?"

"No," I said kind of embarrassed like.

"My gosh! What do they teach you kids in school these days?"

I shrugged as I had no idea. In reality, I had a feeling I probably had been taught about it, but just not retained it due to the fact I didn't pay attention too well. That was the story of my life. School and my brain just didn't seem to get along.

She rubbed her temples with the tips of her fingers and asked, "Do you know what depression means?"

I did know that. "Real sad."

She nodded. "A lot of people were real sad during the Great Depression."

"Why?"

"Well, for a lot of reasons really."

"Were you sad during the Great Depression?"

Mrs. Scholes screwed up her nose in thought. "Not really. It was just life. I had some sad moments and some that weren't so sad and some that were downright happy."

"Was losing your farm one of your sad moments?"

She looked at me as if she wanted to say something, but the words just didn't come. Finally, she nodded.

At the time, I thought I saw a sense of loss in her eyes. I remember wondering if she had lost more than a farm during the Great Depression. I didn't ask at that moment, but I wondered.

CHAPTER 13 – PANTHERS AND BUNNIES

My home on South First Street was only a couple of blocks from Memorial Field and that was pretty awesome because that's where the Norfolk High School held their home games. I loved football then and I still do now, but my parents said I was too young to walk to Memorial Field by myself and watch the games. I was in the sixth grade by then and responsible enough in my opinion, but they wouldn't budge on their position.

So, I found myself in need of a chaperone. My parents were unavailable to do the job and this was a game I really wanted to see. So naturally, I turned to Mrs. Scholes.

"Please Mrs. Scholes," I begged. "I'll even pay for both of us to get in."

Well, in response, she laughed so hard that she nearly fell off her back porch. "Don't you have friends your own age to go see the game with?"

I thought about this momentarily before answering. "No."

Believe it or not, this was a true fact. That fact should have probably depressed me a little, but it didn't. I had a best friend after all. Who cared that she was old enough to be my great grandma. Plus, because of her age, my parents would allow her to escort me to the game as she met the criteria of being a responsible adult.

"Ah, come on," I pleaded with my most whiny of voices. "You've got to come with me."

"And why is it exactly that I have got to come with you?" she smiled as she asked.

"It's only the biggest game of the season," I lied. It wasn't the biggest, but it was pretty dang big.

"What makes this one so great?"

I let my hands flop to my side as a show of my shock that she didn't already know why it was so great. "Because the Norfolk Panthers are having an awesome season and I really want to see them cream the pants off the Benson Bunnies."

"Who are the Benson Bunnies?" she asked.

"They're from Omaha, a real tough team to beat, but I know we can beat them."

"They don't sound tough," she answered. "Who ever heard of a tough bunny?"

"Don't let the name fool you," I answered with a scoff. "Trust me, this is a game you'll want to see."

"No," she said with a scoff of her own. "This is a game I think *you* want to see and I have a suspicion you need me to come along so your parents will allow you to go."

"No!" I gasped as I feigned a hurt look. "What would make you say such a thing?"

I looked at her, expressing as much shock as possible, hoping it was enough to hide any evidence of my underlying guilt concerning my lie. I virtually held my breath in anticipation of her answer.

"Well, for one thing, your mom talked to me earlier today about how much you wanted to go to this game, but that both of your parents had other obligations and couldn't take you."

I felt my face burn red. I'd been trapped in my lie and saw no way to squirm free.

Mrs. Scholes' grin expanded as she continued. "And then she further told me you were not allowed to go alone." Her smile was now stretched to the point of rupture. "She said you were too little."

"I am not too little!" I said hotly.

"Well," she chuckled. "That's what she told me anyway."

I was so annoyed my cover had been blown, not to mention I was being treated like a little kid. Grown-ups could be so aggravating.

"Of course I am free tonight…"

Stupid grown-ups.

"And since we are such good friends…"

Stupid-stupid-stupid!

"I suppose I could let you tag along with me to the game."

I had been so busy being angry and inwardly degrading adults I hadn't, until that moment, registered what she'd been saying. Now however, it was beginning to sink in. I wondered if I'd heard her correctly. Was she actually offering to go to the game with me? Her friendly smile confirmed I had indeed heard correctly.

"Thanks. Thanks a lot," I said with a timid tone.

"You are most welcome," she answered as she patted my back.

*

The quickest way from Mrs. Scholes' house to Memorial Field was through the alley.

By that route, I could make the trip in about five minutes. Of course with my much older and much slower friend in tow, the journey would take considerably longer. I had anticipated this and therefore made sure we started out early. Still, I was anxious to get there. I wanted a good seat to see my Norfolk Panthers beat those Benson Bunnies.

Deep down I knew Mrs. Scholes wasn't trying to drive me nuts with her incredibly slow pace, but she did nonetheless. I swear, a turtle passed us by as we traveled down the alley. *Lucky turtle.*

Well, we eventually made it to the ticket booth which was just outside the stadium and, true to my word, I paid for both of us out of my allowance savings. Of course everything evened out when Mrs. Scholes insisted she buy me nachos and soda. She didn't have to insist too hard.

The nachos were mediocre at best. They weren't what I would consider real nachos. It was simply a clear plastic, flimsy disposable bowl filled with mildly stale corn chips and a separate compartment filled with warm, oozy, orange goo.

The label on the machine that dispensed the goo into my container indicated it was supposed to be nacho cheese. In my opinion the accuracy of that label was debatable. I thought it looked more like golden snot. I thought back to a time I had eaten what I considered to be real nachos back in New Mexico. Apparently, nachos were not well regulated as far as uniformity and consistency across state lines.

Still, I never really could say no to treats regardless of quality. Plus, Mrs. Scholes did owe me for allowing her to tag along not to mention covering the cost of her ticket.

Despite our less-than-stellar pace, we were able to get our tickets and our pseudo-grub with enough time to spare so as to get good seats. We got a piece of prime real estate butt-space smack dab in the middle of the home section of the bleachers with fifteen minutes to spare before kick-off.

Those fifteen minutes seemed to take forever to tick by. In fact, I'd begun to wonder if time had stopped. I didn't wear a watch back then so I had no real way of knowing for sure. If however, I went by the congeal rate of my fake cheese, then time was moving just fine.

Finally, after what seemed to be an eternity, we stood with our hands over our hearts as the national anthem played. Then the teams rushed onto the field. I whooped and hollered as the announcer read off the list of the Panther players. I did not whoop or holler for any of the Bunnies.

I felt a little bad about not cheering for the other team, not really bad, but a little. After all, such actions were not very sportsman like. Still, I heard lots of whoops and hollers from the visitor bleachers when the Bunnies took the field so I felt everything was even Steven.

I ate my golden snot/impostor nachos. I drank my soda. I cheered when we scored. I huffed when we fumbled. My greatest accomplishment came at half-time. The Panther cheerleaders organized our section of the bleachers to do the wave, and miracle of all miracles, I got old Mrs. Scholes to join in.

To this day, I don't remember who won that game although I'd like to think Norfolk did. It's funny to think back now on how I thought that game was so important at the time, yet now-a-days I don't even remember who the winner was.

I just remember what happened after the game. Those post-game events will be forever engraved in my mind.

CHAPTER 14 – POST-GAME EVENTS

When we had walked to the game, it had been a nice early-autumn afternoon. The sun had been shining, a slight breeze had been blowing that just barely hinted at the winter that was soon to come.

There is a saying among Nebraskans. It goes something like this: If you don't like the weather, stick around a few minutes, it will likely change.

Well, that was exactly what happened. While the Bunnies and the Panthers battled it out on Memorial Field, the sky had its own battle between the blue/clear and the grey/cloudy. During most of the game, blue/clear was winning. Then, about halfway through the fourth quarter, grey/cloudy began to dominate.

It started innocently enough as just a small, grey splotch in the western sky. That splotch quickly became a monster. By the end of the game, the blue/clear had been defeated; completely wiped from existence. Only grey/cloudy remained and with its opposition gone, it took the opportunity to darken and deepen. I remember looking up and seeing an ominous churning within its depths as if the heavens were alive and ready to devour the whole town in one massive gulp.

The rule was and always had been this: nothing stops football games in Norfolk, not rain, not snow, and not wind. The only exception to this rule related to lighting. Almost omen-like, the first bolt split the sky as the time ran out on the clock.

The lighting struck. A deep roar of thunder quickly followed. The game was over. The crowd quickly exited Memorial Field. Everyone wanted to get home before the deluge was released.

The parking lot was half empty by the time we got to the exit. I looked down at Mrs. Scholes ancient feet as they shuffled along and was reminded again of the top speed she was capable of. I recalled the turtle that had passed us by on the way here. *Lucky turtle.*

While most people were pushing toward their cars, we pushed in the direction of the entrance to the alley that led us home. This was a task made tougher by the fact that we had to go against the flow of the crowd. By the time we got there, what had been bad, had become worse.

The wind strengthened, picking up the alley's dust and kicking it in our faces like a bully at the beach. Those sandy particles stung my skin like angry little bees, but we had no choice. Our route home required us to endure the sandblasting.

We could have walked half a block further and taken the sidewalk that ran along First Street. I considered this only momentarily. Even though that route would have been void of the alley dust, it also meant walking half a block further. At Mrs. Scholes' elderly pace, who knew how much longer this would take. So, with time being of the essence, we entered the alley.

The plague of dust quickly ended as the plague of rain began. The first drops fell large and fat upon the ground, exploding on impact and creating little wet craters in the alley's dirt.

The wind increased and split the large rain drops into tinier, faster moving, and more numerous droplets. These felt like tiny darts as they smacked onto every exposed inch of my skin.

As painful as the scourge of dust had been, I now wished for it over the rain. For one thing, the rain stung me as much as the dust, but now as the floodgates opened further, I began to feel smothered. Every breath I took seemed to be half water and I began to pray that my lungs would become gills.

We pushed forward against the wind and rain and I found myself wishing we lived in the opposite direction. I had no doubt my old neighbor could virtually sprint if she was being pushed by the force of the wind instead of having to push against it.

As it was, her forward momentum almost ceased to be measurable. I grabbed her tightly around the arm and tried to pull her along, but the increase in speed was miniscule.

I heard a wailing above the din. The tornado sirens were sounding. *Crap.*

Mrs. Scholes was shouting something to me, but although we were only inches apart, her voice was stolen away by the wind, rain, and sirens. I could see her lips moving, but it was like watching an old silent movie minus the normally ever-present, climax-provoking piano music.

I tried to urge her on, but my stubborn mule of a friend planted her legs into the alley mud. She yelled, this time directly into my ear. I caught enough of her words to get the gist. What I heard chilled me more than any drenching of autumn rain ever could.

She wanted me to leave her and get myself to a safe spot. I shook my head. *No way Jose.*

I pulled at her again, trying to yank her forward. She could be so obstinate.

I yanked again, and this time she went along with me. Once more we were off, racing down the alley at the break-neck speed of a lethargic snail.

The roar of the wind overcame the scream of the sirens. I felt Mrs. Scholes duck as she clung to my arm.

Out of the corner of my eye, I caught something fly just over her head, missing me by inches. It blew by quickly, being there one moment and then gone the next; a blur of debris. I was not sure what it was, just a pink mass. It might have been a pastel painted mailbox. It might have been one of those flamboyant flamingo yard ornaments that were so popular at the time. It might have been the pink teacup poodle puppy who lived four houses down the alley. What it was didn't matter a whole lot. What mattered was that if it had hit us, it would have been painful to say the least or deadly at most.

The rain continued to fall in a great torrent, but it no longer seemed to fall downward. It mostly blew horizontal, and at times those raindrops seemed to actually fly upward; flooding my nostrils and making me gag.

The deluge was so intense I couldn't see down the alley more than a few feet. The only way I even knew I was still going the right direction was by looking down at the ground and differentiating between the tannish mud of the alley and the almost black mud and green grass that denoted the edge of the residential yards that bordered it.

A few feet from the edge of the alley something moved. I looked.

It was a swing set. Its swings were angled towards me under the power of the wind. They seemed to be reaching for me as if they were the tentacles of a giant squid that had somehow managed to hitch a ride up from the Gulf of Mexico via the Mississippi/Missouri/Platte/Elkhorn river route.

I stared at that squid that was a swing set. I recognized it and my heart sank. It was one that stood in a yard, only a few properties down the alley from Memorial Field. We had traveled far less distance than I'd hoped. We had a long way to go.

"Crap! Crap! *Crap!*" I screamed as the seriousness of our situation really sank in.

The wind then did something I didn't think possible. It blew still stronger and sounded even louder than before. The sound of that gale reminded me of a freight train.

A terrifying piece of information entered my brain, some tidbit that had actually stuck in there; something I had learned in school of all places. *Tornadoes sound like freight trains.*

"Holy cow!" I shrieked.

A tree nearby uprooted itself. This was no sapling, but a mature elm. We stumbled back. It fell and missed us barely, landing across the alley and blocking our escape home. A flash of lighting ripped the sky into jagged fragments. The crack of thunder that followed, boomed over everything else.

We stood there in the alley, huddled together. I could feel her shaking.

I didn't know what to do. At Mrs. Scholes top speed, it would take an hour past eternity to get around the fallen tree and twice that long if we decided to climb over it.

The lightning flashed again and in its brilliance I saw something I hadn't before. We were not alone in the storm.

A figure, dark and tall stood near us. He wore a black vinyl raincoat that flapped in the wind like bat's wings. The coat's black plastic hood was pulled tight over the head and tied securely so the lower part of the face was hidden. Only the eyes showed. Those eyes frightened me beyond words. They were not human.

They were black and bulbous like an insect's. The eyes along with the fluttering black coat reminded me of numerous characters I had seen throughout my days as a 1980s comic book aficionado. This was not the picture of a hero, but of a hero's nemesis.

The figure drew closer and I realized the eyes were not eyes at all. They were dark tinted goggles like those worn by motorcyclists to protect their eyes from the onslaught of dirt and insects that pummeled them as they flew along on their respective iron horses.

The figure was much larger than we were. It descended upon Mrs. Scholes and took hold of her.

Typical, I thought to myself. *Villains always go for the weak link first.*

I didn't know what evil this newcomer had planned. What I did know was I couldn't let him harm my best friend.

Unfortunately, I was no match. I took a swing, my best swing. He dodged it and I hit nothing but air. That was when I realized the stranger wasn't harming her. He was trying to help.

He was pulling her along, around and past the fallen tree. I caught up to them and took her other arm. Together, we dragged her down the alley at speeds I was sure she hadn't attained on her own since the day she stopped driving.

My body ached like a son of a gun, but I didn't give up. I couldn't give up.

That was when all chaos broke loose. The wind changed direction.

First it blew one way, then another, and then another. Then it seemed to come from every direction at once.

I tried to keep focused. I tried to stare down the length of alley, but my eyes felt perpetually blinded by the wind and rain.

In reality, I didn't need to see what was coming. I knew what was coming. I could feel it in my bones. It was the tornado!

The bug-eyed stranger moved between myself and Mrs. Scholes. He had her in one arm and myself in the other. He was strong. I could feel his strength as he tugged me along.

He half-pulled and half-carried us to the side of the alley. The wind was now completely insane. The freight train rumble was overwhelming. The tornado was near.

He tossed us into a drainage ditch at the edge of the alley. I landed stomach down in the muddy water pooled at its bottom. Mrs. Scholes landed beside me with a splash. I looked up at the stranger. His black coat fluttered wildly in the psycho-wind as if it were trying with all of its might to struggle free from the one who wore it.

He dove down on us. My world became instantly dark. He had us under his coat and the blackness therein obstructed my view. He pulled us both into him as a mother hen would pull in chicks under her wing.

We waited in our dark cocoon. I remember feeling the heat emanate from this stranger. I remember the mixed scent of perspiration, vinyl and wet grass. I remember the ferocious pounding of my heart.

There was a brief moment, when everything seemed to slow down to the point of freezing solid in both time and space. I couldn't see much, only the underside of that black raincoat. The flapping of that coat, which up to that point had been loud, quick and insect-like, now sounded lower in pitch and slower in its flapping. It was less the frantic hyperness it had been and now appeared more like the graceful waving of a large flag caught by a gentle breeze.

In that moment of stillness, I felt a strange sense of clarity the likes of which I had never before experienced. It was a moment I will always remember. It was a moment when a portion of the little boy in me fell asleep and some of the man I was to become awakened.

That strange moment passed as quickly as it had arrived. The scene resumed its normal hectic speed, but that brief slowdown had changed me. I was not who I had been, at least not exactly.

The tornado passed. I could hear it still raging, but the freight train was departing for other destinations.

Our protector jumped up and was gone as quickly as he had appeared, in the blinking of an eye. I crawled out from the ditch and hauled

Mrs. Scholes along with me.

The nearest house was missing half of its roof. Bits and pieces of the missing half could be seen in misshapen chunks scattered as far as the eye could see.

The storm was blowing itself out. We stumbled the rest of the way home. Neither of us said a word. I knew it was a solemn moment and I suspected she thought the same.

A part of me, the boyish part that had not yet given way to the man who had recently awakened, was dying to ask her who that stranger had been. In the end, I remained silent.

Deep down, I knew who it was that saved us on that crazy autumn late afternoon. I didn't need to ask her. I simply knew. It was her elusive but ever-present guardian angel.

CHAPTER 15 – FINALLY, NO MORE BOLOS

By the spring of 1986, I was in the ninth grade. Nothing had really changed for me. Well, I guess one thing had changed. My mom had finally given up on making me wear bolo ties to school.

That was a good thing. A kid my age in 1986 wearing a bolo tie – well that was just plain weird. Not to mention it would simultaneously attract bullies and repel girls which were two things I didn't need any help with.

I didn't need that kind of heat, so the ties got packed away in a box labeled 'Nostalgic Memories' and put in the attic's secret room much to my mother's disappointment. I didn't want to disappoint my mother, but she just had to get it through her head that I was growing up.

Besides the lifting of the bolo tie dress code, everything else that mattered was pretty much the same. Sure, I was older, and changing; but I still struggled in school and my best friend was still Mrs. Scholes.

As I look back on it now, it saddens me to admit that by 1986, I had given up on even asking my neighbor to come to church with me. It still bothered me that she seemed so content in pushing God away, but I didn't know what to do about it.

I had also pretty much stopped pestering her on the topic of gypsies. The subject intrigued me, but the subject's expert seemed to be the most tight-lipped. Even with church and gypsy history lessons out of the equation, we did a lot together.

I still helped her in the garden. In fact, I had become somewhat of a pro and had been promoted from fertilizer duty to planting, weeding, and harvesting.

I still walked with her to the store and I still pulled the cart so she didn't have to. I thought about the future of this task. Once I got my license in a few more years, I would permanently put that cart out to pasture and just drive her.

The least favorite of my jobs was shoveling snow with Mr.

Scholes. It wasn't that I hated the work per se, but Mr. Scholes was so quiet, creepily quiet. He never spoke and I never saw more of him than his eyes as they looked at me through the sockets of that ski-mask.

Mrs. Scholes' boy was a hard man for me to like. I was a talkative guy after all and it was difficult having all of those one-sided conversations as we shoveled together.

I wondered what Mr. Scholes' story was, I mean his real history. I wondered why he was so quiet and why, as far as I knew, he only came over to shovel his mother's walk, when apparently he lived so close by. I wondered if it had anything to do with losing their farm back in the Great Depression. I wondered if it had anything to do with the taboo subject of gypsies.

Over the last couple of years, Norfolk deteriorated further. Farms were still being repossessed by the banks. Out of work farmers were still moving to town, looking for employment opportunities that simply did not exist. On top of that, a huge migration of urban laborers came to work in the new meat packing plants that had opened recently.

Our neighborhood saw some of the greatest changes. We lived in the old part of town, and as such it was the area of town easiest to find cheap rentals and low-income housing.

Most of these newcomers were good folk who had just fallen on hard times. As good folk, they kept their dignity and morals. There were a few however that dove into the darkness of depression. Those few often self-medicated with legal and sometimes less than legal substances.

When I was younger, I used to walk freely to the movies, or the store to buy something with my allowance. I still did those things, but now I did them with a wary eye. The neighborhood simply wasn't as safe as it used to be, end of story.

I was glad I was there for Mrs. Scholes during those years. I wasn't sure if she noticed the change in Norfolk as it became less innocent. In a way, it didn't matter if she noticed or not. I knew her well enough to know she would continue either way, walking to and from the store with her purse hanging from the handle of her pull cart.

I always went with her on these errands. Just like old times, I went to keep her company and to pull her cart so she didn't have to; but now, I also went as an escort for safety.

I was getting older, and all of those years of shoveling snow and working gardens had served me well in building upper body strength. I'm not saying I was fit to be the next linebacker for the Nebraska Cornhuskers, but I was no wimp either.

Maybe it was because Mrs. Scholes had lost the farm herself back in the Great Depression. Or maybe she just had a soft heart. Either way, whenever we crossed paths with ex-farmer types along the sidewalk, she would greet them warmly.

It was easy to notice those who had come to Norfolk because of farm closures even from a distance. For one thing, they still looked like farmers. They all wore seed company hats and work-worn clothing. It was about a fifty-fifty split between those who wore steel-toed work shoes and those who preferred the more traditional cowboy boots. Many also wore little leather pouches on their belts that I later found out held pliers and/or pocketknives.

I rarely saw one smiling. I suppose they didn't have too much to smile about.

Still, Mrs. Scholes always greeted them with a smile. Some would nod in response. Some were visibly intoxicated or otherwise high. You could easily tell those who had been self-medicated. They would often-times smile as well, but it was a spooky sort of smile, a smile of sadness if ever such a thing existed.

One day on our way to the store, she greeted one in passing. After he was out of earshot, I got to thinking.

"Mrs. Scholes," I asked.

"Yes."

"How did you get by after you lost your farm?"

Mrs. Scholes frowned. "It wasn't easy. Both my husband and myself had to look for work."

"Did you find any?"

"We did, eventually. Mr. Scholes found work at the stock yards."

"What did he do there?"

"He had to start at the bottom."

"Doing what?" I pried.

She smiled. "Those cows and sows don't use toilets or wear diapers. Somebody had to shovel their stuff out."

"Yuck!"

She smiled more broadly. "Such work didn't bother him. It was a job he was familiar with, coming from the farm and all. We were both just happy to have a paycheck."

"What about your son? Did he have to go to work too?"

"Times were hard. Everyone that could work, did work to help support the family."

"What did he end up doing?"

She seemed to ignore my question and I hoped I hadn't pushed too far. "I'll tell you what I did. I was lucky enough to get a teller job at the only bank in town that hadn't closed up or been shut down by the Great

Depression. The only reason I got it was because my husband had been friends in grade school with the bank's manager.

"Wow, did you know anything about working at a bank before they hired you?"

She shook her head. "Sometimes it's not what you know, but who you know that makes all the difference in the world."

"Did you like that job?"

She shrugged. "I don't know if people are wired to truly like their jobs. I did like keeping a roof over my head and food on the table. So, if that means I liked my job, then I guess I did."

"Was it weird working for the bank that took away your farm in the first place?" I simply had to know.

She shrugged. "Sometimes, you have to forgive and forget."

"I think when I start to work, I'll try to find a job I love."

"Oh, really?" she said through her grin. "And what exactly are you going to do?"

"I'll be your caretaker of course."

We both laughed and she gave me a big hug. It was nice.

CHAPTER 16 – BREAKING AND ENTERING

It was a night I'll never ever forget. For one thing, Norfolk was like a sauna. Record highs were recorded that August of 1986, and the air was so heavy with humidity that you didn't move through it as much as you swam through it. Also, this night marked the beginning of the adventure which is the entire purpose of this diary.

I was sleeping on the screened-in porch attached to the back of our house. Air conditioning wasn't a luxury you could get at the price my parents paid for that house. Therefore this spot was the most tolerable part of the home.

It was hot on the porch, but a far cry from the alternative, of my sweltering upstairs bedroom. A light breeze blew through the open screens which made it feel downright arctic by comparison.

I was asleep. And then I wasn't. Something had startled me. My first thought was that my parents had been out to check on me, but upon inspection, I saw I was alone on that porch.

I looked at my digital watch. The LED lit numbers said 2:20am.

I tried to think on what had woken me up. I thought hard and I realized it had been a sound. It had been the sound of glass breaking.

I looked about. All the windows in the porch were glassless. Only screens separated me from the bugs that were so prevalent that summer.

I was about to go back to sleep having convinced myself the noise was all just in my dreams. Then I heard more.

Somebody was speaking in a whisper outside my summertime bedroom. My eyes popped open, wide as saucers. I lay as still as possible, barely daring to breathe. I hoped the whisper was a figment of my imagination. Deep down, I knew better. I heard it again, short tense whispers. And with that, my hope died.

My curiosity wrestled against my desire for safety. Curiosity won. Like a prowling cat, I scurried from my makeshift bed I had made on a wicker couch to the nearest window screen.

The air was cooler here. It chilled me as the slightest breeze surrounded my sweaty body. I was wearing only boxers.

Although I knew I was invisible within the confines of the porch's darkness, I couldn't help but tremble with fear. I peered out into the night, trying not to breathe for fear the change in air pressure would somehow be sensed by the creeper or creepers who lurked on the far side of my flimsy screen.

I saw nothing. The glare of the sodium vapor lights from First Street didn't reach the back yard. It was nearly pitch black. My pupils were dilated to the max—no need to wait for them to adjust. I just had to wait. I didn't wait long.

One of the darker shadows shifted. I ducked down. My heart was pounding. Somebody was hiding. Somebody hid just on the far side of my screen.

I sat there on the floor, petrified with fear. I couldn't begin to guess how long I existed in that frozen state. Time at that moment seemed inconsequential. My most intense memory of that time was the feeling of my heart pounding against my sternum and vibrating my whole body.

I listened. I heard only silence.

The image of that shifting shadow played over and over in my mind as I sat there in a crumpled heap on the floor of that porch. I tried to tell myself it was probably just some nocturnal animal on the hunt for nocturnal prey. But the more I thought about the shape of the shadow and how it moved, the more I knew what it represented. It was the shadow of a human being.

I tried to convince myself the figure was just Mrs. Scholes. *Sure, that was it*, I thought to myself. *Mrs. Scholes just decided to walk around the outside of her house in the dark in the middle of the night. Right? Wrong.*

I tried to think who else it might be, but nobody came to mind. Then one word materialized into my brain from out of the past: *gypsies.*

Instantly, I wanted to run off and escape to the secret room in the attic and hide behind my box of bolo ties. I didn't act on this thought however.

I couldn't just run away and leave Mrs. Scholes all on her own, not when somebody was lurking about. For goodness sakes, she was willing to fight a rabid dog with nothing more than a broom to help me. How could I abandon her now? The answer was clear. I couldn't.

Slowly, I got a grip on myself and realized what needed to be done. I had to call the police.

Slowly and silently I got up, planning to go inside and make the call. As I rose, I kept my eyes fixated on the dark scene outside of the screened window. What I saw changed my plan.

A light was turned on in my neighbor's house and instantly, a shadow appeared against the drawn shade of her living room window. It was not Mrs. Scholes. It was the silhouette of a man. In his hand, I could clearly see the shadow of a gun.

There was no time to call the police! My best friend was in danger and the police might take too long in getting here. That was a risk that I simply couldn't afford to take.

Almost without thinking, I crept beyond the safety of the back porch. The night air was humid and warm, yet I shivered as I crept closer and closer to her house.

Fear reached its grubby claws in my direction, but I would not and could not let it master me. As quickly as possible, I scurried through Mrs. Scholes' gate which had been left open. This worried me further because Mrs. Scholes never left her gate open.

I imagined bullets leaving the barrel of that gun. I imagined it happening at any moment. Every step I took, every breath I drew in; I wondered if it would be my last. My terror was working hard to pin me down. I had to push through it. I had to help my friend.

I gulped as I slithered up to her kitchen window. My heart was pounding so hard I suspected the beginnings of an adolescent heart attack as I peered into the world of Mrs. Scholes' home.

Something crunched under my foot. It was broken glass. Luckily, the ground was soft and I didn't cut my foot.

I stared through the broken kitchen window. I saw only darkness.

I knew what I had to do. I had no choice but to follow the intruders by the same path they had blazed. I wriggled into the house like a predatory snake. I rolled onto the kitchen sink. Then, as silently as possible, dropped to the floor.

Despite my terror, I was proud. I had entered silently, like a ninja.

A light shone through the kitchen entrance, but anything beyond remained hidden from me. In cat-mode, I stalked ever closer to that entrance until I was just beyond the shaft of light overflowing from the next room.

I listened to the voices. They were low, barely louder than whispers. Still, thanks to the extreme silence of the night, they carried to my ears. I heard everything.

"We just want the Bible," a man's voice said. It was gruff.

"I don't know what you're talking about."

My heart went out to Mrs. Scholes. Her voice sounded so weak and frightened.

"The hell you don't," replied the man.

"I really don't," she whimpered.

"I'm talking about Milo's Bible. Where is Milo's Bible?"

"So, you're Gypsies. I should have known." Mrs. Scholes sounded bitter.

Gypsies? With that confirmed, I wanted more than ever to run and hide, but that was simply not an option. I had to help my friend.

What to do. What to do. I racked my brain until a plan began to emerge. Slowly, I retreated away from the light and back into the darkness of the kitchen. I wasn't running away. I couldn't do that to my friend. I was trying my best to help.

It had suddenly occurred to me that although I felt there was no time to go into my house to call the police, I could do it here. I reached for the kitchen phone, slowly lifting the receiver from its cradle.

My heart skipped a beat as the phone slipped from my sweaty palm. For one eternal moment, I juggled that receiver between my fumbling fingers. If it fell and clattered, I would be a goner. Finally, I gripped it solid and put the receiver to my ear.

I stood there just listening to the dial tone, thankful no one seemed to have noticed my juggling act and also thankful the line worked. If TV had taught me anything, it was that bad guys usually cut the line before breaking and entering. A crucial step had been missed on their part, and it was an opportunity I wouldn't throw away.

Mrs. Scholes had one of those old phones with a rotary dial. I put my finger into the nine-hole and realized just how much concentration such an act took. I found I was too rattled to dial. I took a deep breath and gathered my wits. Finally, after what seemed an eternity, I dialed the three most important numbers known to the phone-dialing community.

I held my breath to the point of nearly fainting as the rotary retracted after each number was dialed. The grind of that mechanism sounded loud in my ears. In reality, it must have been minute because no gypsies came running in to take me hostage.

"Nine-one-one, what is your emergency?" a woman's voice spoke from the receiver. She sounded like she was talking through a loud speaker from my perspective.

I looked towards the kitchen's entrance, but no thug came barreling through the door. Still, I felt dizzy with nervousness.

"Hello? What is your emergency?"

"407 South First Street," I hissed. "Hostage situation, send the police."

"Hello? Please repeat."

I dared not repeat. So far, my presence had remained undetected to the one with the gun. I could not afford to tempt fate.

Directly below the phone was the kitchen trash can. I pushed the foot pedal that operated the lid. It opened. As quietly as possible, I lowered the receiver inside and let the lid close over it so that the cord bobbled to and fro as it stretched from the trash to the wall-mounted phone-base.

I could still hear the voice of the dispatcher, although it was muffled enough I couldn't understand a single word she said. I hoped to God she was getting the message to the proper authorities.

I crossed the kitchen again, painfully aware of the sound my bare feet made as they stuck to the kitchen linoleum with every step. It was not loud, but to me it was like fingernails on a chalkboard.

I turned and looked where I had just stepped. In the dimness, I saw dark spots. Apparently, my foot had been cut after all by the glass outside. I just hadn't noticed with all the adrenaline surging through my system.

Back at the lit entrance to the kitchen, the man's voice became audible once again. "Enough of these games. I am only going to ask one more time. Where is Milo's Bible?"

"And I will tell you one more time. *I do not know*!" I could tell she was trying to be tough, but the tremor in her voice gave away her fear.

I rallied my courage and peeked around the corner. A stranger had raised a gun to Mrs. Scholes' head. His thumb was cocking the hammer back. That's when my instincts kicked in.

What happened next will always be etched into my permanent memory. I remember sprinting into the room like a Spanish bull in first sight of a matador's scarlet cape. I remember seeing the man's expression of shock as I barreled in. I remember the gun swinging. I remember it turning to point at me! I remember grabbing it around the barrel, trying to reposition its trajectory. And I remember the gun firing.

The boom was deafening, much louder than any of the guns fired on *Maverick*. Of course, Maverick never fired his gun right next to my ear.

I brought my knee up into the man's giblets. I brought it up as hard as a frightened kid can when charged up with piss and vinegar. My knee came up. The man went down. The gun fell to the floor. That's when I noticed the second man. Unfortunately, I noticed him just a smidge too late.

The guy tackled me from behind. I went down hard and felt the breath escape my lungs with an audible rush of air.

I couldn't breathe. I could feel the weight of the attacker on my back. I opened my eyes. The gun was right in front of me. I grabbed the weapon, but couldn't roll over to get a shot. Holding it backwards and above my head, I pulled the trigger.

That bullet must have missed because the man didn't fall off of me.

Instead, the kickback of the weapon sent it flying away from me to clatter to the floor. At the same time, I felt the other's elbow rain blows on the back of my head.

I managed to grab the gun again. I turned it backwards again. Being the slow learner that I was, I pulled the trigger again, but either the chamber was empty, or it had jammed. I had no idea which. My entire gun expertise rested on TV western shows after all.

I heard the man howl in pain. This confused me. I was pretty sure I'd missed with the gun. It was then that I caught Mrs. Scholes' reflection on the wall mirror in front of me.

She was kicking my assailant in the same spot I had used to down the first man. Her kicks were not as strong as mine, but what she lacked in power, she made up for by repetition. *Go Mrs. Scholes.*

Suddenly the room became very crowded. The Cavalry had arrived, or more precisely; the Norfolk Police.

My plan had worked. The dispatcher had traced the call to Mrs. Scholes' house. That, in combination with the ruckus of gunfire, had given them probable cause to force an entry.

They swarmed the scene. It was a welcome swarm. The melee was over.

CHAPTER 17 – HERE COMES THE CAVALRY

It's no fun having a knee rammed into your back while your arms are being cuffed behind you. Still, I was glad the police had arrived.

They kept yelling at me to stop resisting, but I was hyped up on adrenaline by that point. That, combined with my age, made it difficult to relax.

The next thing I knew, I was being pulled to my feet and made to stand next to the two intruders. That was the first time that I got a good look at them.

The tall one was wearing bib overalls with no shirt underneath. He was also wearing an old Cargill Seeds cap that had seen better days. One would think he was a farmer except he had no pouch for his pliers or pocket knife so I saw through his disguise. Plus, Mrs. Scholes had already identified the duo as gypsies.

The other one was shorter, plumper, and looked stupider than the first. I had a feeling he was more of a tagalong than the brains of the operation.

The noise was distracting to say the least. The police were shouting. Mrs. Scholes was trying to shout over them. The only ones who were quiet were the two intruders and myself.

I could hear bits and pieces of what Mrs. Scholes was trying to communicate to the men in blue. She was trying to explain that I was not one of 'them,' but the cops either weren't paying attention, or simply didn't care at that moment.

Mrs. Scholes began to shout louder, but the cops said they would address everything shortly. Right now, they had to secure what they kept referring to as 'the immediate crime scene' and gathering what they labeled as 'primary evidence'.

Eventually, of course, they released me. It was probably a good thing they kept me restrained for a bit. It gave me time to calm down. Maybe that was their goal all along. Maybe that was something they were taught at the academy. Who knows.

My parents were quite shocked to be woken up to banging on the door and an identification of authority. I suppose no parent wants to open their door in the middle of the night to see their son standing between two police officers and wearing nothing but a pair of boxer shorts.

"Oh my gosh," my dad said. "What's he done?"

I was a little perturbed that my dad's gut reaction was to assume I had gotten myself into some kind of trouble. I was a good kid most of the time and had never broken any law. So why would he automatically conclude I had been doing something I shouldn't have been?

I was too worn out to protest his apparent lack of trust in me, but was irked nonetheless. However, once the police explained what had happened, his attitude changed, and consequently so did mine.

The police kept referring to me as a hero. At this, I laughed. I only did what Mrs. Scholes would have done for me, if the situation had been reversed.

I was still in shock over the whole incident. Who would break into an old woman's home anyway? She was so old. And she wasn't rich so what would they steal?

I smirked as I thought about that. She really didn't have much of monetary value. What she did own, I was sure the thieves wouldn't want. Still, in my mind's eye, I pictured the shorter one wearing Mrs. Scholes's old terrycloth robe and the taller one decked out in her pink hair curlers and pulling her prized grocery cart.

Mrs. Scholes had stood back in our front yard, away from the whole midnight-family/police reunion, presumably to give us space. Now, I turned to her and invited her to stay at our house for the rest of the night, but she politely declined, citing the fact that the police were still investigating the crime scene and she wanted to stick around in case they had questions for her.

I gave her a hug and told her good night. What she whispered in my ear while in mid-hug sent chills down my spine.

"Don't say anything to anyone about what you heard those gypsies say to me," she said quietly in my ear. "I'll tell you everything tomorrow."

The rest of my night was sleepless for the most part. I didn't spend it on the back porch as it no longer felt safe. I spent those few remaining dark hours in my upstairs room. It was swelteringly hot up there. Still, it was my space of the house and a good place to think. I had a lot to think about.

The remnants of my teenaged adrenaline levels slowly evaporated and I finally drifted off to sleep as the sun crept above the horizon. Luckily, being summer vacation, my schedule was more or less open that morning.

My parents normally disallowed me wasting my summer sleeping in too late, but given recent events, they must have decided they would make an exception. They didn't come in and wake me up, at least not as early as they usually would. For that, I was thankful.

I slept until noon, when a knock on my bedroom door pulled me from my slumber.

CHAPTER 18 – GROCERY DAY?

On some level, I knew somebody was knocking on my door. However, in my sleep-deprived, semi-conscious state, I felt inclined to ignore it.

The knocking was persistent. I continued to ignore it as best I could.

Finally, to my relief, the knocking stopped.

Then, the shaking began.

"Wake up," my mother's voice drew me from sleep. "Mrs. Scholes is here to see you."

My eyes popped open. Mrs. Scholes had rarely, if ever, come over to my house. Usually, it was the other way around.

"Where is she?" I asked as I sat up.

"Waiting downstairs."

"Tell her I'll be right down," I hollered to my mother as she left my room. I forced the fatigue away. Quick as lightning, I was up and dressed; 1985 apparel head to toe.

I came down the stairs looking like I had entered a Magnum P.I. lookalike contest with white shorts and a Hawaiian-print button-up shirt with white Reeboks on my feet. I lacked Tom Selleck's mustache and couldn't grow one even if I'd wanted to. Also, I didn't have Magnum's gun.

Given the events of the previous night, I wouldn't have minded having that weapon. Then again, given my firearms training (which was nada), and considering how well I handled the gun the previous night (which was embarrassing to say the least), I stood a fair chance of shooting myself where it counts if I had that gun jammed into my belt like the famous Hawaii sleuth.

At the bottom of the stairs was Mrs. Scholes. She looked nothing like a character from Magnum or any other 80s TV show.

She had the seemingly perpetually present pull cart with her. She evidently had pulled it up our porch steps and into our house as if leaving such a valuable item outside would have invited thievery. Then again, given the deterioration of our neighborhood and the events of last night, maybe her concerns were valid.

"Did you forget?" she said to me with a barely noticeable wink.

I had no idea what she was talking about.

"You forgot?" she said as she put her hands to her hips.

I just stood there trying to fully wake up and make some sense of her gibberish.

"You forgot," she said again.

I just stared at her.

She sighed. "You were going to go shopping with me today."

"For groceries?" I asked. It was not her grocery shopping day.

"Well, I don't have enough money to buy Mr. T's gold. So, I guess I'll have to settle for groceries."

Mrs. Scholes had never before used a 'Mr. T.' reference that I was aware of. Things were just getting weird.

Puzzled, I followed her out the door, pulling her old cart with me and eating a banana my mom handed me on my way out. I waited until we were on the sidewalk and safely out of my parent's ear shot.

"So, why all the espionage spy shit…"

"Shh," Mrs. Scholes interrupted.

Shushed by Mrs. Scholes? I thought to myself in disbelief. *What was the world coming to*?

"Firstly," she whispered to me. "Watch your language. Secondly, if we are going to talk, let's do so quietly. Who knows what eyes are watching and what ears are listening."

I looked around but saw no one else, just us.

"Don't look so unnatural," she hissed. "And don't look directly at me when we talk. Let's act like we're casually walking to the store."

"But we *are* casually walking to the store," I answered, a little concerned that the events of the previous night had triggered some sort of dementia in the brain of my neighbor.

We walked toward the store and she said nothing for a block. Finally, I could take the silence no more. "So, are you going to spit it out or what?"

"I'm just trying to figure out what to say and where to start."

I said nothing in response.

After more silent moments, she spoke. "My son is dead."

"What?" I turned toward her.

Her eyes were wet. Tears were running down her old cheeks.

"I told you not to look at me when we spoke," she said through a sob.

I looked away. "How?" was all I could manage.

"The gypsies got him."

I tripped over my own feet and nearly face-planted myself on the sidewalk in shock. *The gypsies got him? What the…*

CHAPTER 19 – THE CON

We walked slower than usual to the grocery store so she could tell me all she had on her mind. By the end, I was dumbfounded.

*

"My son has been dead probably for half a century."

I did some quick math, "Since 1935?"

She nodded. "Give or take."

"But I shoveled snow with him just last winter."

"That wasn't him," she sighed. "You were shoveling snow with me. You've always shoveled the snow with me."

I shook my head. It just wasn't possible. Was it?

"Didn't you ever wonder why he—I mean I—never spoke?"

"You told me he was just a quiet guy."

"Didn't you ever wonder why he always wore that ski mask?"

"It was cold. I thought he liked to keep his face warm."

Despite her tears, Mrs. Scholes chuckled. "Dear boy, I believe I've duped you."

"But why?" I asked.

"Do you remember back when we first met and you asked me if you could shovel my sidewalks?"

I did. I nodded.

"Well, back then I didn't know if I wanted a friend like you. No offense, but it had taken a long time for me to get used to being alone in this world and I was scared to change. So I told you my boy shoveled for me so you would not."

I grinned. "Looks like things backfired on you."

"So it seemed, and once I started the lie, I had to continue. Lies are like that, easy to start, but hard to reverse once they get rumbling along. But I want to be very clear, I don't regret for a moment that you were so persistent. I loved all those times shoveling with you."

I glanced at her briefly even though she had told me not to look at her. Her eyes had taken on a faraway look and I knew she was no longer with me in the present, but visiting memories from her past.

"Yes, 1935 was about the right year, give or take a few."

"During the Great Depression?"

"Yes."

"When you lost the farm?"

"Just before we lost it."

I nodded.

"That was the year Milo met Tabitha."

"Who's Milo?"

"That was my son's name," she said with a half sob/half laugh.

"Oh, I never knew his name."

"Well, it was Milo."

"Who was Tabitha?"

"She was the damned gypsy witch who tried to steal my son away."

"Oh."

She paused. "As a rule, I believe people are born equal, with at least some capacity for good regardless of their ancestry."

I nodded.

"Now having said that, you must know that for every rule, there are exceptions. Hitler, Vlad the Impaler, and Jack the Ripper come to mind. And then, there's Tabitha in a category all her own."

"So, Tabitha was a gypsy witch?"

Mrs. Scholes chuckled a cold chuckle. "Those are my words. She would have called herself a gypsy princess. She led that particular group of gypsies around our neck of the woods back then. Whether or not her followers were as evil as her, or if they simply followed some code of loyalty to their leader, I could never figure out. Regardless, I told Milo to steer clear of her, but did he listen? No, he did not. I can't say I blame him. Milo was eighteen and Tabitha, despite her other shortcomings, was beautiful."

I squinted my eyes, trying hard to picture her in my head. I had no idea if I was right on the money or way off base, but I kept getting a picture of a girl at school who had dressed up as a fortune teller last year at a Halloween party.

"Tabitha kept coming around flirtingy and distracting Milo from his chores. My husband sent her away on many occasions, making it clear there were rules for courting. Milo would call on her if he was interested."

"Was he?" I had to ask.

"Aren't you listening? I told you he was eighteen. I told you she was beautiful. What do you think?"

My face had suddenly become very warm. I wondered if I was blushing.

"My husband, Milo, and myself—we all had a little talk. Two out of the three of us did not like Tabitha. Her kind were not trustworthy after all and we wanted to make it clear to him she did not meet our approval."

"Her kind?"

"I stand by my statement: all people are born with a capacity for goodness. Still, we have free will and choose good or evil. Those were different times. Perhaps it would be frowned on to say today, but *those particular* gypsies chose to follow evil. They couldn't be trusted any more than you could trust a coyote to guard a chicken-coop."

"Did Milo stay away from her then?"

She sighed, "If he had, maybe he would be alive today."

I wasn't following, but my curiosity kept the questions coming. "Why didn't he listen?"

"Again, he was eighteen. She was beautiful. You're a teenager now, what would you have done?"

I knew the correct expected response would have been that I would obey my parents, but I said nothing. Truth be told, I didn't know what I would have done.

I liked girls, sure. But I had yet to have an actual girlfriend. That was probably a lingering effect of my sorted bolo tie wearing past, a preconceived barrier I would need to overcome unless I could find a girl who had the same attitude towards bolos as my mother—which I suspected and actually hoped was highly unlikely.

"No," she mumbled. "He did not stay away from her."

"They were in love then?"

"No, they were not in love! Milo may have thought he was, but what they shared was not love. He was infatuated with her, but she was using him like the con artist she was."

"What happened?"

"She got him alone once out in the woods down by the river. She had lured him there under false pretenses."

"What then?" My curiosity had reached a crescendo.

"Not any of the hanky-panky you're probably thinking about in that teen-aged brain of yours."

"Hey," I said, a little miffed.

"I know what boys your age think about, so don't act innocent. This, however, was 1935. People led very different lives back then, especially when it came to matters of sexuality."

I felt embarrassed and wasn't quite sure why. "How do you know what did and did not happen out there?"

"I wasn't there of course, but I believed my son and he said nothing happened."

"How can you be so sure?"

Her voice cracked as she answered me. "Because he was my son. Also, he had proof."

I said nothing. By saying nothing, I was hoping to speed things along. I wanted to know how the story ended; nay, I needed to know.

"The whole thing turned out to be a trap," she blurted.

"A trap?"

"Yes. Out there in the woods, he suddenly found himself surrounded."

"By who?"

"By her family, of course. Who else?"

I nodded.

"They ruffed him up a bit. It wasn't a total thrashing. They wanted him to be able to walk back home, after all. They needed him to be the messenger. Tabitha herself gave him the note to deliver along with a slap to his face."

"She didn't really like him?"

"It was all a scam."

"What did the letter say?"

"It was a pay-off note. It said that they wanted five hundred dollars, or they would accuse Milo of having his way with Tabitha."

"What? But he didn't do anything like that, did he?"

"Of course not. He knew he didn't and we knew it, too."

I said nothing as I thought on this. I tried to put myself in Milo's shoes and shuddered.

"Back then, there were no DNA tests. It was harder to prove innocence. And those were different times. Even having sex before marriage was enough to get you ostracized from the community."

"So you paid them the money to keep Milo's reputation safe?"

She nodded. "Even so, it was no easy decision. It was the height of the depression and we were barely scraping by as it was."

"But you had to do it, didn't you?" I asked as I thought of my own parents and how I knew they would do just about anything for me.

"Of course we had to do it," she answered without hesitation.

I felt my blood begin to boil. I never thought I could get so angry about something that had occurred so long before I was even born, but here I was.

"We sold some hogs. We sold them at a loss so we could sell them quickly. The gypsies gave us two days to get the money together; only two days, no more."

"Why so little time?"

"We found out later they were getting ready to move on. They were gypsies after all, that's what they did. They had to move onto other scams and new victims."

"If they were leaving anyway, do you think they would have followed through on their threat?"

She shrugged. "There's no way of knowing. It was a risk my husband and I were not willing to take. Plus, we had no idea at the time that they were getting ready to leave. Her family in particular were opportunists. Sometimes they stuck around if they saw profit in it."

"Hindsight is always twenty-twenty," I said. That was a statement I had recently learned and was quite thrilled I had the chance to use it in everyday conversation. I hoped I had used it correctly.

"Exactly," Mrs. Scholes responded, confirming my hope.

"So," I said, sensing there was more to the story. "What happened next?"

"Milo, and only Milo was to bring the cash to the same spot in the woods down by the river from when they gave him the note and the black eye."

"Just him?"

"Yes."

"Wasn't he scared?"

"I imagine he was. He didn't say he was, but who wouldn't be?"

"I know I would have been scared out of my mind," I said.

"If he wasn't scared, I more than made up for the difference. I was plenty scared for both of us, I can tell you, and that is a fact."

"He was walking into a very dangerous situation," I commented.

"Yes he was," she said as her voice began to crack.

"This was a life or death situa…" I suddenly stopped talking as the realization hit me that this was no Hollywood movie script. This was a true story, one I sensed did not end happily. Furthermore, this was a story very close to my friend's heart. "I'm sorry, Mrs. Scholes."

"It's okay. I was the one volunteering this story. It's one I've had bottled up inside for way too long, and now you've become involved, it's one you need to know."

Involved? I wondered what she meant by that. *How had I become involved?*

"So, as I was saying, he went alone."

I gulped. It had all happened way back in the 30s and yet at that moment, I found myself drawn in, fearing for Milo's safety.

Then again, I was apparently, 'involved' so maybe this wasn't as much in the past as I thought. Maybe this all went deeper than I could imagine. Maybe I was in too deep for escape. I gulped again. She continued.

"He followed their instructions. I accompanied him as far as the edge of the woods. Then I let him go on by himself. Watching him disappear into those woods was one of the hardest things I ever had to do in my entire life, I can tell you that."

I found my cheeks were damp. I wiped them dry with the back of my hand, but they became wet again in a matter of seconds. *Stupid tears.*

"I told him I would wait for him right at the edge of the woods."

"Where was your husband?" I had suddenly noticed he was absent from the story line.

"Farming doesn't give you a day off very often. He left at the crack of dawn, saying he had chores to attend to."

"Oh," was all I said in response.

I wondered how a father could go off to work knowing his son was entering a dangerous situation, but I guessed if I had asked that question, Mrs. Scholes would simply tell me that those were different times. She seemed to throw that logic at me often.

"So Milo entered the woods carrying a burlap sack full of cash," she continued.

"Five hundred bucks?"

She nodded. "Yup. And believe me, five hundred dollars was worth a lot more back then than it is now. Today, that would be about four thousand dollars, give or take a few."

I let out a whistle.

"Believe it or not, that's when things went from bad to worse."

Given how this story was going so far, I believed it.

She continued. "The gypsies were there waiting for him. They demanded the money. He gave it to them. He was trying to cooperate, but that wasn't enough for those scumbags."

I had never heard Mrs. Scholes use the word 'scumbag' before.

"Pardon my French, but that was exactly what they were."

I never understood that phrase 'pardon my French'. Usually when somebody used it, the word they had said was not French at all. In this case, I was pretty sure 'scumbag' was not French nor was it all that crude as to invite the 'pardon my French' statement, but like I said, I couldn't recall her ever using that word. I suppose to her, it was quite vulgar indeed.

"One of those scumbags pulled out a knife."

"But he was cooperating!" Being entirely sucked into the story, I felt the need to defend him. "Were they going to stab him?"

"Hard to say why they did what they did. Maybe they were going to kill him. Maybe they were just trying to scare the ever-living piss out of him. That's a question I still don't have the answer to."

I was in shock. I was in shock that there was such evil in the world back in 1935. I was also shocked that Mrs. Scholes used both 'scumbag' and 'piss' in the same day – *pardon her French*.

"Why don't you know?" I asked. " What did they do?"

"I don't know what the man's intentions were with the knife, because he dropped dead before he could do anything with it."

This story just kept getting stranger and stranger. "What??"

"He had been shot."

"Shot?"

"Yup, right through the head."

"Who shot him?"

"Well, it turned out Milo's dad wasn't out doing chores after all. He went into the woods early that morning and got a good hiding spot up in one of the nearby trees in order to watch the action and make sure nothing happened to Milo."

"And you didn't know?"

"If I had known, I'd have stopped him and he knew it. He didn't plan to kill anyone. He just brought along his gun to ensure Milo's safety. He did what any father with a rifle would have done when that knife came out."

I knew Mrs. Scholes had told me not to look at her as we walked along. I wasn't sure why she had been so adamant on that. In my mind, she was being a bit paranoid. Regardless, I broke the rule. I looked at her, I couldn't resist.

Her face was ashen. Her skin was wet with perspiration. Her breathing was loud and heavy. She continued, unaware I had broken the rule, or perhaps no longer caring.

"The gypsies scattered as my husband dropped from the tree and ran toward Milo."

She looked ill. "Mrs. Scholes, are you okay?"

She nodded. "What I've got to say, I've got to say. It's been penned up inside me way too long."

Nevertheless, I was worried for my friend. The stress of telling her story didn't seem to agree with her.

Her voice cracked. "Milo wasn't hurt. The man that pulled the knife wasn't hurt either."

"He wasn't?"

"Nope. Like I said, he was dead and dead people don't feel pain.

Ergo, he wasn't hurt."

"Holy shit!" I said using my own French.

"The remaining gypsies grabbed the money and fled into the woods."

I noticed our pace had slowed. In fact, we were barely walking anymore. The reason was clear. Mrs. Scholes was lagging.

She began to sob as she continued talking. "From some unseen spot in the woods, a gunshot boomed. Apparently, one of Tabitha's family had a rifle of their own!"

"Did they shoot Milo?" I asked suddenly recalling the fact that Mrs. Scholes believed her son was dead.

She shook her head.

Process of elimination struck. "Your husband?"

"I heard the shots from where I waited and came running."

As she spoke, I noticed how her eyes seemed so sunken into her face and how hollow her cheeks appeared. Perhaps, it was just the light playing upon her aged face, but she looked skeletal; her skin like bleached bone against the glare of the summer sun, her teeth glimmering from bared lips.

"When I got there, the gypsies were gone and so was Milo. My husband however was in no condition to go anywhere."

She put her hand to her chest as she spoke. *A broken heart?* I wondered. Or perhaps it was something more.

"He was still alive, but just barely. He told me everything."

We were no longer walking at all. We were simply standing on the sidewalk. Mrs. Scholes seemed to vibrate with an inner energy. I didn't feel it was a good energy.

Her voice was raspy. "Where was Milo? I kept asking him. Where was Milo?"

"Where was he?" I needed to know, too.

"Milo went after them. He took his daddy's rifle and went after them!"

Mrs. Scholes definitely didn't look well. The hand on her chest was white except for the blood vessels that spider-webbed her skin in purplish-blue lines.

"That was the last thing he told me before he passed!"

Then, as if there was simply nothing more for her to say, she collapsed to the ground.

"Mrs. Scholes!" I screamed.

Her hand remained on her chest, but had become a gnarled fist clenching a handful of her blouse. It looked less a hand and more the claw of a dying creature.

I screamed for help. I screamed like a banshee.

CHAPTER 20 – THE AMBULANCE

Calling for help in 1986 was no easy task. There were no cell phones back then. You had to get to a land line, or just scream and jump up and down until somebody took notice.

The nearest payphone was at the 7-11 down at the corner of First Street and Norfolk Avenue. That was a block away, which was too far.

Sure, I could have sprinted that distance in a minute, but that would have meant leaving my friend alone. That was something I just could not do.

Frantically, I tried to flag down cars as they passed on First Street. The first few drove by and my heart sank. Perhaps I looked a bit too frantic. Or perhaps there was something unsavory about a kid dressed like Thomas Magnum.

Every car that drove by was a jab to my gut. I tried hard to memorize the face of each driver as they passed. I was not a violent kid, but if I recognized them later—well let's just say I would not be in a condition to be held responsible for my actions.

Behind me, Mrs. Scholes moaned. It was not a normal sound. I feared the worst.

Out of options, I thought of how Mrs. Scholes had risked her life to save me from Jake. Focusing in on that thought, I took a deep breath, rallied my courage, closed my eyes and stepped right out into on-coming traffic.

I refused to open my eyes. I refused to open them when I heard horns blaring. I refused to open them when I heard tires screeching. I refused to open them when I heard a line of expletives coming from an angry man. In fact, I must have fallen into a state of shock, because I don't remember opening my eyes until the ambulance arrived. When I did finally look, the scene before me froze my blood.

Paramedics surrounded Mrs. Scholes where she had fallen on the sidewalk. There were so many of them, so many that I couldn't see my friend in their midst. One of them kept turning and asking me questions.

"Do you know this person?"

"Yes," I said. I was surprised at how disconnected my voice seemed as I heard myself talk. It all felt like a bad dream.

"Were you the one who called 911?"

"No."

"What is her name?" the paramedic asked indicating Mrs. Scholes.

I told them. They called to her, but with all of the chaos, I couldn't tell if she responded.

"What's her first name?"

It never really bothered me before, but now I found it irritating that I actually didn't know her first name. For all I knew, she didn't have one.

"What's her first name?" the paramedic said again, this time more urgently.

"I don't know!" I shouted. "I don't know her first name!"

It all felt so fake, so much more than what mere reality could dish out. Yet, here I was, engulfed in this horrible situation. All I knew was that Mrs. Scholes couldn't die. She simply was not allowed. *She was my best friend!*

I watched as they worked on her. They had some sort of a tube inserted into her mouth. They kept putting things on her chest and yelling 'clear.' I knew enough to know such procedures were not good signs.

"Mrs. Scholes!" the paramedics shouted repeatedly. "Stay with us, Mrs. Scholes!"

The day was hot, but I shivered. The day was sunny, but I felt a blanket of darkness descend upon me. *Please God, don't take Mrs. Scholes*, I prayed silently. *Please God, she is my best friend.* I suddenly remembered my mission, *I still need to get her to church.*

I prayed this over and over with complete sincerity knowing God always answers prayers and hoping He would answer mine quickly. I prayed. I shivered. I cried.

CHAPTER 21 - HOSPITALS

The ambulance's back door opened and appeared to suck Mrs. Scholes into it along with the stretcher that she rode on, a team of paramedics, and a conglomeration of assorted medical equipment. The door shut behind her entourage and the ambulance tore down the street. Its lights flashed. Its siren wailed. Then, it was gone, and so was she.

I was stricken with an odd numbness as I stood there all alone. I knew the day was hot, but I couldn't feel the heat. I knew I should be sorrowful, but I only felt malaise. I was without being, existing only in the flesh.

I walked home, pulling Mrs. Scholes' cart behind me. One of the wheels was rusty. It squeaked as I pulled. That noise sounded as forlorn as I felt.

I listened to that off-key squeak. I knew it should have irritated me the way it screeched as I pulled that cart along, but it didn't. It sounded so far away and I was too disconnected to care.

I left the cart in our front yard, leaning it against the side of the house. Then I staggered my weary body inside.

I remember thinking Mrs. Scholes would never approve of me leaving her prized possession out front for any passing hoodlum to spy and steal, but at that moment I felt too drained to care.

I entered the house and faced my parents. I will always remember the expressions on their faces as I told them what had happened. Their unified look of horror froze upon their faces as if they had suddenly morphed into Gothic stone gargoyles on an ancient spire.

If they only knew the rest, I thought to myself. I neglected to tell them anything about Tabitha or Milo, or that whole mess. I only told them what had happened to my best friend.

I stopped talking and waited. After a moment, as if the gothic gargoyle spell had broken, my parents came to life, shouting questions and wanting answers. I didn't feel like talking about it and gave only basic responses.

I wasn't put off by their interrogations. I knew it just meant they cared about me and my friend. I had always known I had been blessed with good parents. Their actions just reinforced what I already knew.

They offered me a ride to the hospital so I could see her, but I declined. I needed time to think. To do that, I needed to be alone. I told them I was happy walking.

They insisted they drive me. I insisted harder that I wanted to walk. They offered to walk with me. I insisted I go alone. Finally, they relented.

One of the great things about smaller cities like Norfolk is that you don't need a car to get around. You could get where you needed to go simply by putting one foot in front of the other.

The town only had two small hospitals. One was a Catholic facility, the other was Lutheran. I had no idea which one Mrs. Scholes would be at. She didn't attend church after all. I had no idea which denomination she would identify with or if she was in a state of mind to tell anyone even if she did.

I tried to decipher which hospital was closer to the spot where the accident had occurred, thinking the ambulance driver would get her to the nearest, but for the life of me, I couldn't figure that out. Math was not my strong suit after all and I was always stumped by those story questions about trains traveling in opposite directions at different speeds.

I reached the Catholic hospital first and inquired at the information booth. The booth was manned by a volunteer, a girl I recognized from school who was two grades ahead of me.

She opened a large three-ringed binder and scanned the patient listings. Luckily for me, the 1980s were before the time of strict information privacy regulations so I had no problem finding out what I needed to know. Mrs. Scholes was not a patient there.

I left the Catholic hospital in my dust and headed toward the other. Suddenly, a morbid thought hit me. *What if she was not a patient at either hospital? What if she was instead a resident in the morgue?*

Instantly, the other hospital felt so far away. I began to run toward it. I began to sprint.

CHAPTER 22 – VISITING HOURS

As it turned out, Mrs. Scholes was not dead. She was, in fact at the second hospital.

Although it was true she was alive, it was also true she was not far removed from death. The first thing I thought when I saw her was how terrible she looked. Her eyes were closed and had dark circles under them. Her breathing was rhythmic, but shallow. Her hair was matted and lifeless. Her skin was paler than ever, and that was saying something.

I entered her room and listened. All was quiet except for her breathing and various quiet beeps and buzzes coming from a machine that seemed to reach for my friend with countless wire tentacles.

The machine reminded me of something out of an old *Star Trek* episode. I wasn't Captain Kirk however, and the hospital was a far cry from the starship *Enterprise*.

As quietly as possible, I sat down in the only chair the room offered. It was nothing special, just a simple folding chair with a padded seat. I quickly discovered the chair's padding did little to nothing in the way of adding comfort. Within minutes, my legs began to tingle.

I became frustrated as tears blurred my vision. I was somewhere in that process of morphing from a boy to a man, and I knew men didn't cry. Still, despite my protests, the boy in me dominated and the tears came. Regardless of my opinion at the time of what constituted a man, tears rolled down my cheeks. I wiped them away with the back of my hand only to find more were coming. *Stupid tears.*

Eventually, with the back of my hand lacking the absorbency I needed, I got up and retrieved a tissue from the box on the table beside Mrs. Scholes' bed.

"Quit carrying on like that."

I nearly jumped out of my skin as I zeroed in on the voice. It was Mrs. Scholes! Her eyes were open. She had a barely perceptible grin on her thin lips.

"I ain't dead yet," she said with a raspy voice.

"I know that," I answered with a smile I was sure did not look convincing.

"The doc says I am going to be A-okay."

"I know that too," I lied. I had not yet spoken to or even seen a doctor.

Her eyes grew solemn and her wisp of a smile faded away. "If I recall, before this little unexpected interruption, I was telling you about my history with the gypsies."

I nodded, thinking it was strange how Mrs. Scholes picked up her story as if the interruption had been nothing more than a gnat buzzing in her ear or a small child tugging at the hem of her dress.

"What was the last thing you remember me telling you?"

I thought back. "Milo was hunting down the gypsies with his dad's rifle."

She nodded slowly, evidence that her memories were returning. She wrinkled her nose in thought.

"Don't tell me this now, Mrs. Scholes. You need to rest in your condition."

"My condition?" her voice suddenly strengthened. "I'm as fit as a horse. Now listen to me because what I have to say is important. Your life depends on it as well as mine."

My life? Suddenly I was very interested in hearing her out.

"This story all ties into what happened the other night at my house."

I nodded, indicating I would like her to proceed with the story. Now that lives were on the line (namely mine and Mrs. Scholes') I no longer felt her condition should stop her from telling me what she wanted to say. In fact, I now encouraged full disclosure.

"So, Milo took off after Tabitha's gypsy band," she began.

I noticed the constant beeping from her heart monitor quickened slightly at this statement. I wished she could wait to tell me the story, but she was so insistent and with our safety apparently in jeopardy, I was reluctant to stop her. Besides, I was sure a nurse or doctor would tell us if it became crucial for her to take a break.

"He tracked them along the banks of the Elkhorn. There were a lot of trees and tall grass along the river's banks back in those days before the levies had been built. So he was able to follow them under good cover and undetected."

I noticed a slight twitching in the facial muscles of Mrs. Scholes. She was on the edge and her condition did not help. Still, I said nothing to stop her.

"He followed them to their camp. It wasn't much, nothing more than a few jalopies with ropes tied between them and an old tarp flung over the ropes for a makeshift shelter. Back then we called places like that Hoovervilles."

"Hoovervilles?" I repeated.

"Such places were named after Herbert Hoover who was president of the good old U.S. of A. when the Great Depression hit. A lot of us blamed him for the poor economy, so calling such shanty-towns by his name made people feel better somehow."

I saw a tremor in one of her hands. I took hold of it to calm her. It felt as if I was holding a dead fish, cold and clammy. I wanted to let go of it, but didn't for her sake.

"Hoovervilles were pretty common back then. This was just one of many."

My own hand began to shiver at her tremors as if touching her completed some sort of electrical circuit. It made me uncomfortable. I let go. Her hand fell back to the bed.

"It was right out of the pages of *The Grapes of Wrath.* Did you ever read that book?" she asked me.

I shook my head.

"Read it and you'll get the idea of what the Hoovervilles were like."

"Okay." I had seen a copy once before, and remembered it being as thick as a phone book. I didn't have any real inclination to read a book that thick unless it was required in school (which it probably was) or had lots and lots of pictures (which it probably did not). In my friend's current condition however, I felt it best to be as agreeable as possible.

"These people made the rest of us look like royalty. They didn't have a pot to piss in I tell you."

"Why would you want to do that anyway?"

"What?" she asked, annoyed I had interrupted her story.

"Piss in a pot."

She chuckled dryly. "Believe me. We used to do our business in a lot of things before the days of indoor bathrooms. You would too if the alternative was going outside in the cold of winter or the heat of summer or in the middle of the night. Now, listen up because we don't have much time and you're getting me off topic."

"Sorry," I said. I thought it had been a valid question though.

"As I was saying, they didn't have a pot to piss in, but they sure as heck had some money."

If they had money, then why didn't they purchase the all-important piss-pot, I thought to myself, grinning at the inside-of-my-head humor.

As if Mrs. Scholes could read my thoughts, she added "Of course, they had only recently come into the money. They had no chance whatsoever to use it for anything, and that included purchasing a pot to piss in."

"Are you talking about the five hundred bucks they stole?"

"Well, I ain't talking about winning the lottery, but there was also a lot more than what they took from us. Turns out they had used that scam repeatedly and successfully and had accumulated quite a nest-egg."

"Tabitha had been a busy girl," I said.

"Indeed she had been."

The suspense was killing me. "Did Milo get the money back?"

She nodded, but the expression on her face told me there was more to the story.

I watched her closely and concentrated, telepathically requesting the additional information. Who knew if that would work, but apparently it did because she continued.

"He got all the money. He stole back the whole wad."

Suddenly I realized a hole in her plot. "But Mr. Scholes got a job later in Norfolk. You said it yourself, *cows and sows don't use toilets or wear diapers.* After you lost the farm your husband went to work at the stock yards remember?"

She shook her head. "I am afraid I made that up."

I thought of another hole. "How do you know all of this happened? You weren't there." I was so hoping such a tragic story had somehow been simply made up inside of that old brain of hers.

Mrs. Scholes smiled a sneaky smile, building up the suspense. She opened her mouth to speak, but just then we were interrupted.

A nurse opened the door and leaned in. She looked at me with a polite, but firm expression. "I'm afraid visiting hours are over for Mrs. Scholes this afternoon. She needs her rest."

No! I thought. In the words of Paul Harvey, *I needed to know the rest of the story.* I opened my mouth to ask for five more minutes, but before I could say anything, the nurse spoke again. "You can come back tomorrow, isn't that right Mrs. Scholes?"

I looked at my friend, using my eyes to plead with her. *Five more minutes. That's all I need. Just give me five more minutes.*

"I guess we'll have to talk later," she said with a shrug, not getting my message. But her expression showed concern. "Stay safe until we talk again."

"You can't argue with the doctor's orders," the nurse said in an irritating sing-song voice.

Of course you can argue with the doctor's orders, I thought, but didn't say it. Instead, I got up and headed toward the door.

As I passed the nurse and entered the corridor, my courage rallied. I turned back to my friend, jammed my foot into the closing doorway, and asked "How do you know all of this?"

"Because I saw Milo a few weeks later," old Mrs. Scholes said with a tired sigh. "He told me everything."

The nurse nudged my foot out of the way and closed the door.

CHAPTER 23 – A HIDDEN BIBLE

I walked home knowing I should feel exhausted, but such was not the case. My adrenaline was surging and I knew I would be unable to sleep that night. The story Mrs. Scholes told seemed like a script for a TV show. It most certainly didn't seem real. It couldn't be real. Could it?

The whole thing made me nervous. What made me the most nervous was that she had indicated her fifty-year-old story was connected to the recent break-in—and that our very lives were in danger.

I wondered if this whole thing wasn't the product of Mrs. Scholes' aged brain. It was possible, I conjectured, that she was just going senile. At least it was a possibility not to be overlooked.

Senility wasn't out of the question, but one thing made me lean towards believing what she said was true. It was a feeling I had as I walked along. I felt watched. It was more than just being watched. I had the feeling I was being followed.

Whoever it was, I wanted to catch red-handed. Time and time again, I spun around and looked behind me as I walked along. Time and time again, I expected to catch a stalking gypsy, but every time I looked, I came up empty. I was alone as far as I could tell.

I supposed it was possible I felt this way because Mrs. Scholes had placed the seeds of paranoia in my brain, what with her talk of gypsies and how I was now involved. In fact, it was more than possible. It was likely.

Regardless, I couldn't shake the feeling I was not as alone as I wished to be. That feeling stuck with me all the way home.

I ate my supper and then spent time with my other best friend, the good old television. I tried to lose myself in the alternative worlds the TV offered. But neither *Magnum PI*, or *Simon and Simon*, or even *Cheers* could cheer me up.

I needed to escape this mood. It was a strange mood to be sure, a combination of wonderment and fear.

I found myself asking how Mrs. Scholes' story ended and found I was annoyed with the nurse who had prevented me hearing it. I had the uncanny feeling I was somehow a part of that story now. And maybe the ending of the story had not been told because it had not yet occurred.

I shivered as I thought of this prospect. I hoped the story would end well. I feared otherwise.

Despite my fears and despite fearing I would not be able to fall sleep, I slept deeply. In fact, I fell asleep before even saying my prayers. In retrospect, that was probably a good thing because I had a lot to pray about and it would have taken quite a while and I really did need to sleep.

I suppose God overlooks such infractions, at least that's my hope. I recalled that the disciples kept falling asleep when Jesus asked for only one hour of prayer. That was just before his arrest. If he could forgive them at that crucial hour, I suppose he could forgive me as well.

Apparently, the adrenaline in my body dried up as I collapsed onto the bed. It seemed I closed my eyes for only a moment, but when I opened them again, the morning sun was peering through my window. I walked over to that window so I was engulfed in the rays. It felt good to warm my body in this way. I could tell the day would soon grow too hot for comfort. Such were summers in Nebraska.

I dressed quickly. I grabbed an apple and a piece of beef jerky for my breakfast. Then, I was out the door and on my way back to the hospital to visit my old friend.

I knew my parents would not worry about where I'd gone. My dad was at work. So was my mom. My dad had had a job for as long as I could remember. My mom, on the other hand, had only started working a couple of years ago down at the Truck Haven Truck-stop and Café.

So, I was pretty much left to my own devises these days. Some kids might have used such freedom for mischief. I used it to spend time with my elderly friend.

I ate the apple, pitched the core and devoured the jerky in two carnivorous gulps as I walked to the hospital. It was no breakfast of champions, but it was adequate for what my body craved. Nowadays, something like that would sit like a rock in my gut, but not then, when I had a teen's stomach that seemed to be made of titanium and immune to such culinary combinations.

Again, as I walked, that unsettling feeling crept in. Somebody was watching me. Somebody was following. Just like before, I spun around. Just like before, no one was in sight.

The tension of what I was sensing made time flow faster and I found myself entering Mrs. Scholes' hospital room in what seemed mere minutes after I had left my house on First Street. In reality, I knew I had not entered some cosmic wormhole or unknowingly folded the very fabric of time and space.

No, the clock was ticking along at its normal speed. It was simply the pace of my personal life and the fact it had suddenly been plunged into a hyper-drive that caused this time-speed illusion.

I looked at my poor old friend and she returned the look with a weak smile. I thought she looked better, compared to yesterday, but had no idea if that was the honest to goodness truth or just wishful thinking on my part. I was sure her color had returned a little and her eyes had that sparkle I always remembered. It was the sparkle of youth; that verification she was young at heart, which always looked so out of place in the confines of her aged body.

"How are you?" I asked. My question sounded so cliché as she sat in that hospital bed hooked up to monitors and what not.

"I'm good for now. The nurse gave me some meds that might make me sleepy in a little while though."

I nodded. Then my impatience got the best of me. "So, Milo came home and told you everything?" I even surprised myself at how eager I was to hear more of the story.

"No friendly chit chat today huh?" she said with a little chuckle. "It's all just get down to business, is that it?"

I said nothing. It seemed impolite to say *heck yes, I want to find out what happened.*

"That's probably for the best, given my meds might kick in at any moment, not to mention lives are on the line."

There she went again suggesting the possibility of current imminent danger. I gulped.

"Yes, one day Milo came back."

"Did he have the money?"

Mrs. Scholes shook her head gravely. "No."

"What did he do with it then?"

"Whoa, doggy," she said. This was a statement she had used before at times I was getting ahead of myself. "Let's back up a bit. Remember, he stole the stolen money. Now that is a dangerous thing to do; stealing from thieves. On top of that, he stole it all, not just the five hundred dollars they took from us."

I nodded.

"Those days were not like today. This was Nebraska in 1935. It was a bit more wild back then. The Norfolk police force was small. On the other hand, Tabitha's band were many. In addition, they had connections."

"Connections?" I asked. The word drove a tingling of fear into my body.

"They had connections with organized crime syndicates, international connections."

I gulped, unsuccessfully keeping my fears down. Scenes of old gangster movies I had seen on PBS special movie presentations filled my mind.

"This particular bunch of gypsies were pretty low on the totem pole of crime, but their connections made them infinitely more powerful, and infinitely more dangerous."

"And the police were too small to do much good." I said, starting to see the bigger picture.

She nodded. "Like I said, those were different times. Those were dangerous times."

What an adventure Milo found himself in, I thought to myself. *And he was only a few years older than me at the time.*

"They put a price on my son's head," she said with no more than a whisper.

I felt my eyes widen as if I were more owl than boy. "Did they catch him?" I asked, not really wanting to know the answer. Still, I had to ask. Not knowing was torture.

She shrugged, "I never found out, but back then one never stood much of a chance against the mob. If they were after you, they would find you. Sooner or later, they would find you."

My heart sank as I realized it was far less bad not knowing. Now that I did know, I wished that I did not.

"That day back in 1935 was the last time I saw my son. He said he had to keep running, had to stay ahead of them, safety in movement and all that jazz."

"Still, he risked coming to you that day to tell you."

She nodded.

"He must have loved you a lot."

She nodded again as a rush of tears overflowed her eyes and trickled down her cheeks. "He said he had come back to say goodbye."

The end of her statement evaporated into nothingness as her voice cracked into oblivion. I watched her sob and thought of the statement *time heals all wounds.* What a load of crap.

I did what any friend would have done. I took her into the best hug I could offer given she was all discombobulated with wires and monitors and such. We cried it out together.

"Back then, we was more of the church-going type," she said through sobs. "Milo had been given a Bible on the day of his confirmation. He handed his Bible to me on that fateful last day I saw him. He told me to hide it. He told me where he wanted me to stow it—said it would be so well hidden there, no one would ever find it except me or him. Then he gave me a kiss on the cheek and left my life forever."

We cried together some more, caught in the hug even more intensely than before. It wasn't easy for me. I wasn't the hugging type, but sometimes you need to put your own feelings aside when a friend needs you.

"Why did he want you to hide his Bible?" I asked finally.

"At the time, I just thought it was a precious possession of his that he didn't want Tabitha's heathen band to ever violate."

I thought about the recent break-in. It seemed the gypsies wanted something from that Bible beyond simple violation. It seemed it was a precious possession indeed.

I released her from the hug and stared into her reddened eyes. "Why would gypsies today want your son's Bible from fifty years ago?"

"I don't know."

"Do you know where it is?"

She nodded.

"Do you know why anyone would want it so badly?"

She shook her head, "I haven't a clue, but I know from experience that once these gypsies zero in on something they want, they won't stop until they get it." After a moment of silence, she continued, "I never meant for you to get involved in this mess."

I nodded.

"I'm sorry," she said.

"It's okay. I'm a Christian, remember? I have to forgive you," I said as a smile crept on my lips. "God commands it."

She smiled back. "Well, if God commands it, who am I to argue?"

A germination process was beginning inside of my mind. I was beginning to formulate a plan. "It sounds like the answers to a lot of this mess can be found with Milo's Bible."

"I suppose you could be right."

"And you said you know where the Bible is?"

"Yes."

"Then I should go get it."

She sighed. "It could be dangerous. It's obvious we're not the only ones who want it."

I got up and walked to the window so my back was to her. I didn't want her to see the fear in my face. "Danger is my middle name," I quoted from some TV show I had seen once. I looked out her window. Dark clouds had moved in and gloomed up the day. A storm was brewing.

My plan matured. I would wait until evening here with Mrs. Scholes.

Then, under cover of storm and night, I would retrieve Milo's Bible.

I had a feeling getting that Bible before they did meant safety for us. It meant we would have something they needed, something of value; something to barter with, possibly for our very lives.

I continued to stare out the window. "So tell me, where is the Bible is hidden?"

CHAPTER 24 – A HOUSE BY THE RIVER

Overhead, lightning flashed. The air felt heavy with static electricity, as if it were about to spontaneously combust into an uncontrolled frenzy.

Thunder clapped only seconds after the lighting flashed. The storm was promising to be a doozy.

The first raindrops fell in big lazy blobs that spattered on the ground before being absorbed into the thirsty earth. Then, as if those first drops were scouts sent to pave the way, the rest came. They hit the dry Nebraska ground, too many to count, as ominous as the plague of locusts God unleashed upon the Egyptians to entice Pharaoh to let His people go.

Through all this, I ran along the quickly swelling banks of the Elkhorn River. The normally lazy river had been agitated into a violent serpent. The rain had changed it just like Dr. Jekyll's concoction changed him into the infamous Mr. Hyde.

It was nearly dark as night as I ran. Angry clouds kept the setting sun from shining and what light made it through their blockade was weak and sickly. The light of the dying day took on a greenish tinge as if the world was ill and about to vomit.

I ran onward. I had to fulfill my mission. I needed to keep my promise.

That seemingly perpetual feeling of being watched and followed went with me as I ran. I forced myself not to dwell on it. I couldn't afford to cower and turn back. It wasn't an option.

In the distance, I saw the Gillette factory. I knew then I was not only headed in the right direction, but nearing my destination. I rounded a bend in the river and just like that, the long-abandoned farmhouse came into view. Its silhouette rose above me like a resurrected zombie, dark and foreboding and skeletal. The sight sent a shiver down my spine from the top of my head to the tip of my tailbone. This was Mrs. Scholes' old homestead, the farmhouse lost to the bank during the Great Depression and then forgotten by men and time.

In the gloom and through the torrential rain, the ruins reminded me of Norman Bates' house from the movie *Psycho*. Lightning streaked across the sky above and lit up the land, but no light reflected back from the many windows of the house. All the glass had long been gone from those orifices, presumably shattered by vandals or acts of time.

I stopped and looked up at the monstrous house. It seemed a living thing, back from the dead, unnaturally animated like Frankenstein's monster. It howled as the wind and rain rushed through its nooks and crannies, only adding to my feeling it was a creature alive and capable of vocalizations.

Cautiously, I circled the perimeter of the old house until I found the door. It wasn't easy to find.

The front porch had long since caved in, hiding the doorway under a section of sway-backed, fallen roof. I shimmied my way around the mess and into the house as if I were a worm escaping a hungry robin. I left the storm outside. I entered the realm of the inside which, I would argue, was no more hospitable.

Once inside, my fears escalated. I couldn't see a thing except when the lightning flashed outside. Such moments of sight were fleeting, giving me only the most instant of images before they faded back into mysterious gloom.

Those brief photograph-like scenes only made me want to run back out into the storm. It took all my will power to stand my ground. I had made a promise. I had made it to somebody who I deeply cared for and whom I felt certain cared for me. I was not about to let her down.

I took a step further into the house and pulled the flashlight from inside my shirt where I had been carrying it to keep it as dry as possible. I had, for lack of a better term, stolen it from Mrs. Scholes' hospital room. She had told me the doctors used it to look into mouths, noses, and ears. I hoped it wouldn't be missed, or at least it could be easily replaced.

I was worried that, despite my efforts, it had gotten too wet. I was worried it wouldn't work. I pushed the button. The light came on. I was relieved.

Its small beam cut the darkness like a sword slices flesh. It revealed the house's hidden secrets, but only so far as the beam penetrated. It did little to relieve my fear of being watched and followed.

The house was a wreck. I stumbled over old beer bottles and similar garbage as I advanced into the house. It made me sad to think such a once-happy home had fallen into such disrepair. It was now nothing more than a hangout for deviants.

Luckily for me, the ill weather discouraged said deviants from hanging around on that particular evening. The place was empty except for me, or at least it appeared so.

Thanks to Mrs. Scholes' excellent long-term memory and her detailed instructions, I knew where I was going. Through the garbage, I pushed onward.

Past the living room and into the gutted shell of what at one time was a depression-era kitchen, I moved full steam ahead. I turned left, entered the dining room and aimed my flashlight at the stairs which were right where she said they would be.

I jumped as a huge bolt of lightning exploded outside. The strike had been close, too close for my liking in fact. As the boom of thunder ensued, I tried to remember what I saw in the brilliance of the lightning. I couldn't recall seeing anything of significance, just more of the same: garbage, garbage, and more garbage.

The timing of that lighting had been impeccable. It was as if I were an actor on the set of some old black and white horror flick and the lightning had been written into the script at that particular moment so the audience would see the stairs and experience the maximum chilling effect. This was no movie however. This was real life and this mission harbored real danger. With that in mind, I cautiously ascended the stairs.

At the top was the room I had come to search: the attic.

The steep-slanted roof had held these many years for the most part. Here and there, dripping rain water cascaded down the interior of the roof line and the space smelled of mildew; but on the whole, the roof held back the weather. It was a true testament to old-time carpentry.

"On with the mission," I said to myself as I took a step into the spacious room.

It was a spooky space to be sure. Of course the tempest outside did nothing to make it less so. Almost immediately, I began to wonder what had possessed me to go on this mission, but no sooner had the thought escaped me, than the answer popped up. I was doing it for my best friend's safety, as well as my own.

I felt sure Milo's Bible was the key to bartering with Tabitha's gypsy band. It held secrets they wanted, and therefore it had value to me as well.

I thought back to when our friendship first started and I knew then why I could do nothing less than honor my promise to Mrs. Scholes. I thought of all the times we had shared. I thought about the time, she had risked her life to fight off Jake. I thought about the time we weathered the storm after the football game. We had a history of being there for each other and I wasn't about to change that now.

I stepped further into the attic, shining my beam on the weathered wooden floor. Among the empty liquor bottles and obscene graffiti, I saw what I had been told to search for.

In the far corner of the attic, upon one of the floor boards, was painted a heart. It was not red or pink as one might see on Valentine's Day. No, this one was black as night. The color was a representation of the one who had painted it, or rather Mrs. Scholes' mood at the time.

Contrasted against the aged and weathered attic floor, the black heart was barely discernible. In fact, I would wager I would not have noticed at all if I hadn't been keeping a keen eye open for it.

But I had known. I had been told exactly where to look. I knew what it meant. It was like an X on an old treasure map where X marked the spot.

I approached the black heart slowly and reverently as if it marked a holy man's tomb. As I grew nearer to it, my limbs began to tremble with anticipation.

Earlier that day, as Mrs. Scholes told me about the spot, I had a hard time not dismissing it as a mere myth. As I looked at it now, I knew it was no myth.

Still closer to that black mark, I approached; kneeling no longer solely out of reverence but now also out of necessity. The roof-line slanted down at that corner.

Now I was directly in font the black heart. My flashlight beam centered over it as if it were the main attraction at a three-ring circus. The air felt electrified and I knew it was more than residual static from the lightning storm raging outside.

I felt like Indiana Jones as I knelt over the heart, acting like it was some ancient archaeological find. Barely able to coordinate my fingers due to nerves and the cold, I clawed at the floorboard on which the heart had been painted. I found the board's edge, clumsily. As expected, it was not nailed down. With more effort than it should have taken, I lifted it from its place and peered into the small secret compartment.

At first, I could see nothing. Only the depth of darkness greeted me.

I had re-routed my flashlight beam as the board had been removed. I dared not shine the beam into the hole. It felt disrespectful to do so, as if I were disturbing the dry bones of a long-dead king. Besides, I knew what was there. I didn't have to shine a light on it to know.

As if on cue, a bolt of lightning lit the room. In that momentary brilliance, the Bible appeared.

It was dark in color, almost as dark as the blackness that surrounded it. Still, in that flash of lightning I saw the gold-gilded words that had been printed upon it so many years ago.

Milo Scholes. It read.

CHAPTER 25 - ESCAPES

And so I have brought you back to the beginning, all the way back to page one of this diary. We are now at the point where my terror is screaming the loudest, demanding I put this story to the written page. I am desperate to separate myself from this craziness I have hidden inside for so very long, but this is not an easy thing to accomplish. In fact, I liken it to severing one's own finger or toe. Yes, it can be done but not without excruciating agony and iron-clad resolve.

*

You know this part of the story already so I will only summarize. I am in the attic with Milo's Bible. Two gypsies have tailed me to this location and now, though they are unaware of it, they have cornered me with prize in hand. I take my only chance and dive out the window, taking one of them with me. This act, I am sure you remember, initiates a barrage of bullets, all of them targeted at my body.

To this day, I credit God with saving me from those two men and their deadly intentions. I have no doubt heaven held a meeting and decided to give the one who held the gun a sudden inability to aim. I have no other explanation. The story continues with me fleeing the scene. The Bible is in my possession, and I have an elephant-sized turd of horror weighing me down.

*

I ran through the woods as quickly as I dared considering I had no flashlight to guide my way. I still held the remnants of the flashlight not because I had any intentions of returning the stolen item, but because my fist refused to relax and let the trashed item go.

I lamented breaking the flashlight. I could have used its light to guide me at that moment. Then again, perhaps it was a good thing I didn't have the option. No light made me less visible, and being less visible made me less of a target. Plus, I have no idea how I could have beaten my opponent without that flashlight to bash in his face.

The storm was ending. Now it was little more than a light sprinkle. I tried to hold Milo's Bible close to keep it as dry as possible, but as I ran through the wet foliage I realized this was quite impossible. Still, I tried.

In the distance, a lingering lightning bolt flashed, but the thunder was now only a distant rumble. The storm was definitely moving on. Now that the once-ravenous storm had quieted, I could hear the nearby Elkhorn River raging. It was swollen like a gluttonous python and sounded just as ill-tempered. I kept the river to my right. As long as I did, I knew I was headed back toward town.

My going was slower than I would have hoped. The mud was slippery. Clouds covered the night sky and without starlight, moonshine, or flashlight; the darkness was deep. Furthermore, exposed tree roots and long prairie grass hampered my progress. Plus, I needed to move quietly. Who knew if those from the farmhouse were following, or perhaps the whole tribe was hidden and listening, just waiting for me to stumble into their clutches.

My fear further slowed me down. I feared I would trip and fall into the river if I was not careful. With the Elkhorn in its current strength and me being a relatively weak swimmer, I could ill afford such a fall.

By the time I exited the trees and entered the quiet residential street of Park Avenue which ran along the river on the edge of town, I was in pretty sad shape. The street was deserted which was good. Given everything going on, I didn't want attention from bystanders giving away my position to any of Tabitha's band that may or may not be present.

I stopped and examined myself in the cold glow of the nearest sodium vapor streetlamp. I was pretty much one big bruise dotted with cuts and scrapes and splotches of mud.

I was psychologically beaten up, as well. The last few days had been a whirlwind to say the least. I had defended Mrs. Scholes at the break-in. I'd gotten her help when she suffered her heart attack. I learned about the dangers of organized crime syndicates, and the need to rescue Milo's Bible to barter with said syndicates for safety's sake. And now, to put the proverbial icing on the cake, with the Bible in my possession, I had been shot at.

The idea that those gypsies were after me kicked in another obstacle: paranoia. Behind every tree and around every corner, I half-expected them to be there watching for me and waiting to strike. But every time I rounded a corner or passed a tree, I found the danger was only in my mind—at least for now.

Still, my rampant imagination was grounded in truth. Like some coming-of-age after school TV special, it had been dramatized and hyped up. But, as they say in Hollywood, artistic license had been used, but everything was based on true events.

Those men at Mrs. Scholes' old abandoned farm house were as real as real could get. They were as real as the bullets they had shot at me, and as real as Milo's Bible which I held onto for dear life. The fact was, everything had become a little too real. It was so real I could barely stand it.

I looked down at the Bible in my hands. My life had become a surreal nightmare, yet the fact that I held his Bible was proof enough that the nightmare was not only happening but possibly only just beginning.

My paranoia kept me from going where I normally would have gone. I knew I should have gone to the police, but I wondered how much had really changed with Norfolk's law enforcement community in a half century. Norfolk was still just a small Nebraska city more or less. The police force was still nothing more substantial than what would be normally needed for a town that size. It didn't have the resources to confront a group connected to international crime syndicates. Of this, I was quite certain.

I asked myself a simple question: *Could the Norfolk Police Force protect me and Mrs. Scholes, let alone my family?*

Yes, I had seen enough mob movies to know they'll go after your family if they can't get you. That's mob-mentality 101, plain and simple.

The answer came to me at once. *No, they could not offer the protection we needed.*

So I couldn't go to the police. I couldn't go home. With no other option, I headed back to the hospital.

I went incognito, cutting through the dark of night like a phantom. I didn't take the well-lit sidewalks, but instead cut through dark residential properties, jumping over lawn ornaments and evading the few dogs that were out in their kennels at that late hour. Luckily, all those dogs were either chained, fenced in, or caught by surprise and unable to reach me before I escaped their territory.

I kept to the deepest shadows and frequently checked behind me to ensure I wasn't being pursued. As far as I could tell, I was not.

I was alone. I was utterly alone.

CHAPTER 26 – THE NURSE

I knew my parents wouldn't be worrying about me. They had given me permission to stay with Mrs. Scholes as an overnight guest as long as the doctors gave me the okay. Well, the doctors had not given the okay, but my parents didn't know that and I figured what they didn't know wouldn't hurt them.

What a pile of poop that statement was. There were a lot of things they didn't know that could hurt them. They knew nothing about the murderous gypsies or the group's affiliation with organized crime, for example. I myself had only just discovered this world and was finding it a place that could definitely hurt you, whether you knew about it or not.

My heart raced as I entered the hospital. Sodium vapor lights buzzed outside and florescent bulbs lit the main entrance. The brightness of it all stole my gift of invisibility, which made me feel more vulnerable than ever.

Once inside and traveling down the brightly lit hospital hallway, I tried to see in all directions at once, but I only succeeded in making myself dizzy to the point of nausea. Every sound that echoed down the hall seemed to be a sign of the enemy. Every doorway I passed in that corridor was a doorway to danger. I pressed on nonetheless.

It was after visiting hours. I would have to sign in as an overnight guest at the nurse's station, but when I got there I found the desk unattended. My nerves began to tingle as if I had suddenly been graced with a healthy dose of Bruce Wayne's bat sense.

Every other time I had passed this station, a nurse had always been there. I assumed it was a hospital policy to make sure this station was manned at all times. I stood there, not sure what to do. The only sound came from the buzz of the florescent light overhead. My fear was rising.

"Can I help you?"

I jolted and spun around, using Milo's Bible as a shield. I knew the Bible was inadequate against things like bullets, but it was all I had.

"Are you okay?"

I lowered the Bible. It was just the nurse.

"Who are you here to see?"

"Mrs. Scholes," I answered as I tried to will my heart rate to return to normal.

She nodded pleasantly. I had never seen this nurse before, not that I hung out regularly at the hospital. Maybe she was new, or maybe she was just off yesterday when I visited, or perhaps she only worked nights.

She was pretty, with clear skin, brown eyes, and dark brown hair bound in a ponytail high on the back of her head. I guessed she was in her mid-twenties.

She seemed distracted by the Bible. The moment became awkward. "So, do I need to sign in or something?" I asked.

"Yes, I believe you do need to do that, don't you," she said. She fumbled about the desk, eventually producing a three-ring binder with the big bold label of *Sign-in Log*.

"Um, please sign in here," she said, opening the binder and sliding it over to me. She scanned the page for a moment and then said, "Right here," as she pointed to a blank line on the open page.

This was weird. "I don't have anything to write with. Do you?"

"Oops." Her face blushed. "Of course. Hold on."

She went to searching again, opening desk drawers and scanning the desk top for the elusive writing instrument. She seemed about as organized as me, but then again I wasn't the one given responsibility for manning the nursing station.

But there was more to her than simple disorganization. She seemed tense. I watched her closely. Droplets of sweat beaded on her forehead. Of the two of us, I should have been the nervous one, what with Tabitha's band after me and all. I felt my own brow. It was wet as well.

I found the pen before she did. There were four or five of them sitting in an empty ceramic coffee mug with the name of the hospital on it.

I grabbed one from the mug, signed in, and passed the pen and the binder back to her. "You might want to keep this with the binder," I said indicating the writing instrument I had used.

"Thanks for the advice," she said with a giggle. I couldn't tell if the giggle was meant to be flirtatious or was just embarrassment. Either way, I smiled back and turned away.

"Wait," I heard her call. "I need to know what room number you're going to."

That's when I realized something. "I don't know." I had gone there yesterday, but hadn't memorized the number.

I thought it was strange the nurse didn't know. "Don't you have a listing of the patients and their room numbers?"

She stared at me a moment before speaking. "Yes, of course, but we have to verify that you know where you are going. It's the new hospital privacy rules."

I guessed that made some sense. "Well, I don't know the room number, but I know where it is down the hallway."

"I see," she said. Her flirtatiousness was gone. "Well, I'll just have to go with you. Then when we get there, we can verify the room number together."

I nodded.

Together we walked down the hall. I wasn't sure what was going on, but this nurse was definitely a bit strange. She didn't act very nurse-ish. For one thing, she didn't know her own work station well enough to produce a pen. Secondly, it seemed odd she would leave her station unmanned yet again just to make sure I went to the right room.

"This is my first day on the job," she suddenly said, as if reading my mind.

I nodded, but wondered what kind of hospital puts the newbie alone at a nursing station. Wasn't there some sort of training program? Plus, even though it was just a small town hospital, you would think they had it in their budget to man something as important as a nursing station with at least two employees.

I had begun to suspect this woman had gypsy blood running through her veins. If I was right, then I could not, under any circumstances, lead her to Mrs. Scholes' room. She looked sweet enough, but underneath that smile and perfect skin, I suspected a monster lurked.

I wondered what had happened to the real nurse who was supposed to be on duty. I wondered and worried.

"That Bible sure looks old," she suddenly blurted out.

That statement chilled me, but I couldn't let her see that. "It is," I said, forcing calmness in my voice.

"Where did you get it?"

Her questions had the air of an interrogation. "It's Mrs. Scholes'."

"I see." Her voice sounded as if she did not believe me. "That's not her name on it."

I adjusted the Bible so it was out of her view. "It's a hand-me-down."

"I see," she said again. "From who?"

I didn't like where this discussion was headed, so I changed the subject. "Old Mrs. Scholes can't go a day without reading her Bible."

As soon as I said this, I regretted it. If this woman knew Mrs. Scholes at all, she would know what a lie that was and my cover would be blown. Luckily for me, the woman didn't push the subject further.

The numbers on the doors of the rooms rose as I passed. 112, 113, 114, 115; each one nearer my friend's than the one before.

Suddenly, I remembered what room number Mrs. Scholes was in. It just came to me. She was in 118, but I dared not tell the fake nurse. I wasn't born yesterday after all.

I passed 116 and then 117. A plan was forming in my mind.

I stopped at Mrs. Scholes' room and opened the door. Out of my peripheral vision, I watched the nurse. She seemed to tense as I turned the knob. She was preparing for something.

I opened the door just enough for Mrs. Scholes to see a sliver of my face. My hope was that she was awake and would see I was outside of her room. I opened the door just a crack, but didn't go in.

Out of my peripheral vision I could see the nurse. She was rigid like a marble statue. She was poising for an attack, I just knew it. I prayed Mrs. Scholes would stay quiet.

"Wait, is this room nine-one-one?" I suddenly blared out.

"What?" the nurse responded.

I hoped Mrs. Scholes understood that nine-one-one meant emergency. At her age, in her condition, you never knew for sure. "Nine-one-one," I said again, and then, more quietly to the fake nurse, "Oh, I meant, is this 119?"

"This is 118," she said. Her voice was full of intensity.

"Oops, this isn't Mrs. Scholes' room," I lied. "Mrs. Scholes is in 119. Stupid dyslexia."

Honestly, I was pretty proud of my dyslexia reference. It just came to me and I thought it made my scheme more believable. I closed the door to Mrs. Scholes' room and prayed she understood at least enough to stay quiet. Then, I guided the fake nurse to the next room and hoped to God that 119 was vacant.

My heart pounded. My senses tingled. I put my hand on the door's knob and, using all my control to stop my hand shaking, I pushed the door.

I noticed the nurse tensing again. I opened the door further. I took a step into the room keenly aware she was right on my heels. The bed was empty, but I doubted the nurse could see this, as I was doing a fair job at blocking her view.

"Hi Mrs. Scholes," I said as cheerily as I could, considering the stress I was under.

Everything from that point on became a blur. I remember seeing a gun. I had no idea where the fake nurse had been concealing it, but it was out in the open now.

In a panic, I grabbed for the weapon, redirecting her line of fire.

My ears rang as the gun fired just inches from my face. The room's window shattered as the bullet penetrated the glass and changed it into a shower of glitter that would have been quite beautiful under almost any other circumstances.

The ringing in my ears was intense. Still, I could hear screams of terror. They were coming from 119's bathroom. The room was not as vacant as I had hoped.

We spun around like two lovebirds locked in a passionate dance. I can say however, with complete honesty, that although passion was involved, there was no love in our movements.

She was trying to turn the gun on me, but I kept hold of her wrist with both hands to prevent it. I dared not let go of her wrist, not at any cost.

The gun boomed again, momentarily drowning out the shrieking from behind the bathroom door. The second shot was closer than the first, parting my hair with the speed of sound.

We spun faster. Our legs tangled. We went down together, landing hard.

I felt lucky to have landed on top. Upon impact, she let out a burst of air and a wheeze. At the same time, I heard the gun clatter away along the floor.

I had always been taught never to hit a girl. However, I don't believe that rule pertained when the girl in question was trying to kill you.

I had dropped both the Bible and the remnants of my flashlight when I had first seen the gun. I wished I had held onto the flashlight at least. I had experience using it as a weapon, after all.

Instead, I gave her the best right hook I had in me. Something flew from her face, not bloody-red as I had hoped, but black. I recognized it as a false eyelash.

It fluttered away from her face like a little baby bat. Unfortunately, because of my short attention span, my focus was too much on the baby bat and not enough on my adversary. She caught me hard under the chin.

The blow dizzied me momentarily, but I couldn't afford to be dizzy, not even for a moment. Using my advantage on top, I jumped off her before she could get a second punch in and rolled toward the gun.

I used her body as leverage to slide to the weapon. The barrel was warm and a wisp of smoke curled from it as I picked up the firearm and spun around in true Thomas Magnum style.

I thought at this point I was ready for anything. However what I saw when I turned was a surprise. The fake nurse had bolted. I was alone.

I heard her footsteps echoing down the hall, softer with every repetition. Then I heard them no more.

That is not to say all was quiet. My heart boomed. My breathing was wheezy. And despite the ringing in my ears, I could hear the incessant screaming from the mystery-occupant of the bathroom.

Brandishing my newly obtained weapon as if I were posing for a Charlie's Angels photo shoot, I bolted from room 119 into the empty hallway. I stayed low and close to the doorway in case the nurse's escape had been a ruse. I prepared for the potential ambush, but luckily nothing happened. I left behind the screaming bathroom dweller and went into Mrs. Scholes' room. She was just hanging up her phone.

"The cops are on their way," she said.

I nodded.

"Did you get it?" she asked me.

In my state, I had a hard time comprehending what she meant. "Did I get what?"

"Milo's Bible. What did you think I meant?"

"Yes I got it!" Given what I had been through, I thought a little more patience on her part was in order.

"Well, where is it then?"

"I dropped it in the other room."

"Well hurry! You need to get it and get out of here before the cops arrive."

"Why did you call them if there's such a time crunch?" I asked, a little exasperated.

"Because," she said with a quiver in her voice. "I was afraid you'd been shot."

"Oh, well thanks, I guess." And I meant it.

"No time now for this mushy nonsense. Go get Milo's Bible!"

I ran back to 119. I could still hear the occupant of the bathroom. Her screams had died down to a steady stream of incoherent whimpers. I hoped the poor soul would be alright, maybe after some therapy. Maybe.

I felt a little guilty bringing a totally innocent party into such chaos, but I'd really had no choice. I had done only what had to be done. I wanted, at the very least, to open the bathroom door and apologize, but there was no time to waste. Plus, I had the feeling fewer eye witnesses were better than more. I didn't need people identifying me later in a criminal lineup if I could help it.

It wasn't hard to find Milo's Bible. It was lying on the floor where I'd dropped it, back when the whole melee began. I swiped it up and ran back to Mrs. Scholes.

"Give me a hug," she said.

I hugged her awkwardly. It was more of a sea-lion hug as I had the gun in one hand and the Bible in the other.

"Now get out of here. The cops will be arriving any moment."

"Where am I supposed to go?" I asked, at a loss.

"Look, I've been doing a lot of thinking here in the hospital and I think I know why those gypsies want his Bible so badly. I think there must be some hints in there as to where Milo hid their treasure."

"Okay?" I said it as more of a question than a statement.

"If I'm right, then you'll need to follow the clues Milo left in the Bible. You need to get to the treasure before they do."

"What clues?" This all sounded a little too much in line with standard Saturday morning Scooby Doo episodes to be real. I mean, what's next; Mr. Jenkins accusing me of being a meddling kid as I rip a zombie mask off his face?

"I don't know exactly and there's no time for me to help you figure it out. You'll have to do it yourself. Now scat!"

"But what about you?"

"I'll be fine. Now get going, I'll do my best to talk slow for the police. You'll need every bit of head start you can get."

My indecisiveness must have been evident. The impatience in her eyes was growing by the moment.

"Listen to me," she said. "The police won't be able to protect us forever. They're simply not strong enough, and those gypsies are persistent sons of guns who will stop at nothing to get what they think is theirs."

I looked at the door, but didn't move. In the distance I heard sirens.

"Listen!" Mrs. Scholes sounded frantic. "You're not a child any more, and this enemy won't treat you with mercy. If they catch you, it's game over. Do you understand?"

I nodded.

"You need to keep that Bible in your possession at all costs. Use any clues you find in there that might direct you to the treasure."

"But...." I began.

"Holy cow man! There's no time! Just remember the Bible and the treasure are what the gypsies want. If we can keep those things from them, then we have the power. If we lose them, the gypsies will see us as dispensable. Do you understand?"

I nodded again and ran out the door wondering if it was the last time I would see old Mrs. Scholes. At the end of the hall, I looked back. The police had arrived. I caught only the slightest glimpse of them as I rounded the corner. I didn't think they saw me. They seemed focused on the panicked occupant of room 119. Plus, Mrs. Scholes started screaming for help as well. I would have to thank her later for that little distraction.

I turned away and ran.

Through the parking lot I sprinted. I needed the dark of night to hide me. The lights of the lot made me nervous. I imagined Tabitha's army hot on my heels and armed to the hilt.

At the end of the lot, I glanced back. It seemed like half the Norfolk police force had arrived. Their patrol car's lights were flashing. No ambulance came with them, but I supposed that was because the paramedics were already at the hospital. *How convenient.*

I breathed in a cleansing breath and exhaled. I had escaped. Not a single officer had noticed me.

I shivered as a cold thought entered my mind. If a suspicious boy with a gun could bolt out of a public hospital full of Norfolk law enforcement officers (who had come on a shots fired call, by the way) and run through a well-lit parking lot full of Norfolk police cruisers without being detained or even noticed, how could they keep me safe from Tabitha's band?

Mrs. Scholes was right. They couldn't protect me. I was on my own.

CHAPTER 27 – INSIDE MILO'S BIBLE

I felt sure my heart would explode at any moment from the paces I was putting it through. I was no track star and it showed.

Still, I refused to stop running. I ran through the dark night, keeping to residential backyards and alleys as much as I could.

I wasn't sure where I was going. All I knew was I wanted to get as much distance from the hospital as possible. Sooner or later, the police would start searching for me and I most certainly didn't want to make it easy for them.

The gun I had taken from the fake nurse didn't do much to elevate my confidence levels. If anything, holding a weapon made me even more nervous. With the exception of the last few days, my firearms experience consisted of what I had seen in movies and on TV as well as my extensive use of cap guns that I played with when I was younger. The gun I now held was much more deadly than a cap gun, infinitely more deadly.

As I flew along, I thought of my friend. I had left her behind with only the protection of the Norfolk Police Department, which I had already determined was woefully inadequate to protect and serve against this enemy, who they probably didn't even know existed. I hoped I was wrong in my assessment of Norfolk's finest, but I feared I was dead on the money.

At her age and in her condition, Mrs. Scholes should not be under so much stress. I just hoped the police could protect her long enough for me to find the treasure.

And what will I do if I actually succeed? The thought spontaneously erupted in my brain.

It was a question I had not previously considered. Everything over the last couple of days had gone so fast. I had been too busy surviving to consider such issues.

I was operating on a step by step basis, learning things as they presented themselves and not a moment before, but now the next step had arrived. In the crisp light of the full summer moon that had appeared with the disbursement of the rain clouds, I stopped running and opened Milo's Bible for the first time.

I wasn't sure what 'clues' I should be looking for or if I would know them if and when I saw them. The Bible didn't simply fall open. It had been closed for decades and was used to being that way. I pried it open.

It was then that I discovered the bookmark. The marker consisted of a thick paper material, rigid enough to create a separation of the pages.

I looked at the marker more closely. It was an old black and white photograph.

In the pale light of the moon, the figures in the picture looked ghostly. The photo was faded with age. Regardless, I recognized my friend's smile as she looked out at me from the distant past.

A much younger Mrs. Scholes stood there in the photo. She had been rather attractive back in the day, not like a supermodel or movie starlet, but with a deeper beauty. It was a beauty she still possessed, though these days it was harder to see under the wrinkles and years.

In the photo, she stood with a rugged, handsome man. He wore a hat and even without the benefit of color, I could tell it was well-worn. He wore it low on his head, hiding his face in the shadows of its ample brim. His eyes sparkled from that shadowy dimness. They looked like kind eyes.

Besides his eyes, nothing in particular drew my attention to the man. He looked to be your run-of-the-mill rural Nebraskan, wearing a simple shirt and dark overalls.

Standing in front of the couple and in the center of the photo was a boy. He had thick hair with no part and looked, in my opinion to be about ten years old or so.

I turned the picture over and noticed writing. It looked as if the ink had been there a while. *Proverbs chapter 28 verse 22, then reverse it, chapter 22 verse 28,* it said in oxidized brown script.

It was then I noticed the marker was set to the first of the two indicated scriptures. I read it, then quickly flipped to the second passage and read it as well.

Eureka! My worries I would miss the clue evaporated. Instantly, I understood the hidden meaning. It was not a hard code to decipher if you were familiar with Norfolk, but it was a meaning that the original author of the Proverb had never intended.

I knew what I had to do. I knew where to go. I headed off. Time was of the essence.

CHAPTER 28 – THE EVIL EYE

He that hasteth to be rich hath an evil eye, and considereth not that poverty shall come upon them. That was Proverbs 28:22. Two words had been circled in this scripture: *evil* and *eye*.

As crazy as it sounded, I knew, or at least I thought I knew, what this meant. It was as if I had climbed inside Milo's mind just by holding his Bible.

I ran through the dark, looking back frequently, expecting to see Tabitha's entire horde tailing me, but every time I looked, I wasn't being followed, at least as far as I could tell. I took no chances and continued to run.

I knew I was not the only one interested in the treasure. Those gypsies wanted it as much as I did, maybe more if that were possible. In addition, I knew they pulled no punches and would do anything to get what they wanted.

In this regard, I was at a disadvantage. I had a gun, but I wasn't sure I was capable of using it against another human being. I knew if the tables were turned, they wouldn't hesitate to blow my brains into cranial confetti. I tried to keep this in mind. I tried to prepare myself to become a killer if duty called. Still, deep inside, I knew the truth. I was just a scared kid without a murderous bone in my body.

I made every effort to keep to the deepest shadows as I ran along. I dared not use the main streets, the ones with the city lights. Light was not my friend, at least not at the moment. Even still, I wished for the dawn, not for the light itself, but because maybe dawn would show all of this to be one big old nightmare. I put my hope in waking up. It was a hollow hope.

One piece of knowledge chilled me the most. I knew that before my quest was finished, I would have to enter lit areas of town. Such exposure was not something I looked forward to. Still, I could think of no way to avoid it.

I headed toward Norfolk Avenue and the downtown district. I feared Norfolk Avenue. It was the most lit street in the whole dang city. But I had no choice. Milo's Bible told me I had to.

The Evil Eye Tavern was there, a Norfolk institution. It first opened back in 1932 by a man named Edward Nard. Amazingly, I remembered this from school when we were taught the history of Norfolk that all the local children were required to learn.

Luckily, and against the odds I might add, this was information I had retained, not so much because I was good at learning (which I was not), but more because the man's last name sounded a lot like nerd, and I had an immature sense of humor. Of course the method that helped me retain the information was neither here nor there. The good news was that I *had* retained it and that knowledge had now become extremely useful to me.

Mr. Nard, they said, had named his new tavern as something of a mean joke. The name 'Evil Eye' referred to gypsy superstition. The belief at the time was that if you were a gypsy, you avoided the evil eye at all costs. The evil eye was a malevolent look that caused misfortune to the one onto whom the look was directed.

Therefore, the Evil Eye Tavern catered to the majority of Norfolkians who did not like the gypsies' presence in the town. Mr. Nard, like so many back then, disliked them and named his establishment as he did to ward them off. Sure, it was discriminatory, but it was a sign of the times and the state of the town back then.

Ahead of me in the distance, I saw the light from Norfolk Avenue outlining downtown's buildings and trees. Their shapes stood out black against the phosphorous hue cast by the streetlamps, appearing like a ghost town haunted from within.

As I neared the street, the glow became greater. Details emerged. Leaves on the trees swayed above my head and dripped residual raindrops onto the sidewalk below. A discarded Styrofoam cup rolled along in a curved path because of its slightly conical shape, carried by the light breeze of the waning night.

The light made me uncomfortable. I wanted to turn and retreat to the safety of darkness' cover, but I knew I had to move forward. I had to do it for my own long-term safety and for Mrs. Scholes.

The street was empty. At this hour, even the bars had closed and presumably all of those establishments' employees had gone home. At least that was my hope.

I ventured into the light of the streetlamps and immediately felt the pressure of such exposure pushing down on me like radioactive fallout. If anyone had been following me, I wouldn't be hard to spot now.

Like a mouse looking for cheese, I looked up and down the sidewalk that ran along Norfolk Avenue. Like the mouse, I was wary of the trap such treats commonly were connected to. I saw no trap. Still my uneasiness persisted.

I ran down the street as quickly and as quietly as I could. Still, I felt I was not quick enough nor quiet enough. Once again, I felt the stares of unseen eyes.

I skidded to a stop in front of the *Evil Eye Tavern*. Its entrance had always intrigued me.

The door was of heavy oak. In its wood were carved intricate images of eyes. Some were open and watching, staring out in various directions. Of those that were open, some looked angry, others looked fearful, and a few looked sad.

Some of the eyes were not open at all. Of those that were closed, some seemed to sleep, while others appeared more as if their owners were deceased.

I had always found that door both intriguing and creepy. I could see why some people in town, gypsy or otherwise, did not dare venture through such a doorway or patronize that establishment.

On either side of the massive oak door, were stained glass windows. The windows exhibited similar ocular images. At times, when the sun had set but the bar was open, the incandescent light from inside would penetrate the glass and illuminate those eyes. At times like that, the tavern seemed somehow alive and watching any who dared pass by.

Now however, the lights inside were all off and the many eyes had been darkened. The tavern, if it lived, now slept.

The door would be locked at this hour, but I tried the handle nonetheless. It was indeed locked as I had suspected.

That was fine with me. I wasn't planning on entering through that door anyway. At first, I was tempted. After all, the place had been made to ward off gypsies, which was something I definitely wanted. On the other hand, I couldn't just live there forever, and there was still the issue of Mrs. Scholes' safety as well as that of my parents. Plus, the hair-raising factor of entering through a door of eyes in the middle of the night while being certain I was being followed by Tabitha's bloodthirsty band made me queasy, not to mention the whole legal issue of breaking and entering.

I laughed to myself as I thought about that last issue. Here I was in the early morning hours slinking around Norfolk, a minor with a gun. The last thing, I should have been worrying about was breaking and entering. Still, I didn't need to draw undue attention to myself.

I turned from the tavern to study the street before me. It appeared deserted. Yet I still felt I was being watched and from more evil eyes than those that stared at me from the door and windows of the tavern.

I held the gun tightly and felt palm-sweat ooze from under my tight grip. I placed my index finger on the trigger. I hadn't done this previously for fear I would accidentally squeeze off a round, an act that would surely not end well.

Even if I was lucky enough not to blow myself to kingdom come with an accidentally-fired round, I would still be exposing myself to attention either from the cops, or sleeping citizens, or from the far more dangerous enemy I felt sure watched me even now from unseen hiding places.

My trigger finger was shaky. I had to focus to keep it from shaking too much.

With my free hand, I opened Milo's Bible to where I had left the photograph marker. I read the second passage. I had read it earlier, but now I reviewed it for further understanding.

That first passage had directed me to the *Evil Eye*. The second would guide me to the location of the hidden treasure. At least—that was my hope.

CHAPTER 29 – THE ANCIENT LANDMARK

Remove not the ancient landmark which thy fathers have set. That was Proverbs 22:28.

With the gun in one hand and Milo's Bible in the other, I stared at the ancient landmark. It stood darkly before me like a sentinel created to guard the door of eyes that led into the tavern, perhaps to judge all who entered in order to ensure their worthiness.

The statue gave off the vibe of invincibility, looming larger than life and staring down at me like some all-condemning judge. The sculpture was bronze and in the form of a man. He had been there, as far as I knew, as long as the tavern he perpetually watched over.

One hand was hoisted above his head holding a pint of beer as if he had just exited through the door of eyes after an evening of revelry and had turned to toast the tavern's good health. He faced the door of eyes with his mouth stretched in a drunken grin, proof the tavern's drink was strong indeed. His other hand stretched out before him, pointer finger extended, angled down toward the space directly in front of the door.

All who entered or exited the door of eyes had to pass under that judgmental finger. There was no way around it.

Although he grinned, there was no happiness in his stare. His eyes were dark and piercing, further supporting its role as judge and guard, rather than jester.

The statue itself was the size of a man, but he stood larger than life upon an elevated granite base so that he looked down on all who stood before him. On the base was a plaque. The plaque was brass and, once upon a time, probably shone like polished gold, but through the years, it had become tarnished and dull. Regardless, I had no problem deciphering the words etched into it. In fact, I had read it many times before in passing this way.

Remove not this ancient landmark says the guardian of the door. I welcome those free of the Gypsy curse. Those not under the curse may enter through the door and enjoy the treasure of the Evil Eye.

I read the plaque a second time so as to commit it to my memory. I didn't know exactly the significance of this statement, but it seemed eerily similar to the Proverb from Milo's Bible. There had to be a connection.

I examined the base more closely as well as the plaque that was upon it. The base was massive and narrowed as it rose above the sidewalk, resembling a pyramid with the top removed. Instead of a point, it had been leveled off to where the statue began.

The plaque had been set into the side of the pyramid so that the top of it was flush with the granite itself. It sat at an angle congruent to the base.

I drew closer to the plaque. I felt there was something unusual about it. It held some secret. Again, I felt Milo's knowledge somehow transferred to me through the ancient Bible I held, which he had once owned.

I noticed no screws held the plaque in place. That meant either it was stuck in place by some sort of adhesive, or it was simply sitting in its grooved home, held there by its own weight.

A suspicion entered my mind. It seemed far-fetched, but then again, given what I had already experienced that night, maybe it wasn't so far-fetched after all. Acting on my suspicion, I ran my fingers along the crack between the granite and the plaque. Whether in my head or in reality, I couldn't say, but I thought I felt air flowing along that groove.

I tried to pry off the plaque, which I now suspected was a lid, but it wouldn't budge. What I needed was some sort of lever, a screwdriver or better yet, a crowbar.

Unfortunately, neither screwdriver nor crowbar were to be found. I searched my pockets for an alternative. I pulled out a quarter. I always carried a quarter with me in the event I had to use a payphone. This was, after all, the days BC—Before Cellphones.

I forced the quarter into the groove and pried with all the strength in my fingers. The plaque moved.

It slid up just slightly, but then slammed back down before I could wiggle my way into the crack. This was probably a good thing. The plaque was heavy and I didn't want to risk pinching my fingers.

Unfortunately, the quarter spun out of my grip and rolled down the sidewalk. Like a hungry cat chasing a mouse, I dropped Bible and gun before going after it. I couldn't let this quarter escape. It was my only tool even remotely suitable for removing the plaque I now felt certain was a lid.

Retrieving the quarter, I quickly ran back and re-inserted it. This time, I pried it up slowly. As before; the lid lifted, the quarter slipped, and the lid came crashing back down.

This time though, before the lid fell, I caught a glimpse of blackness.

There was definitely a hollow space under the base of the statue.

Simultaneously intrigued and frustrated, I looked for the quarter again. The coin was grossly inadequate. What I needed was a good crowbar.

"Looks like you could use a crowbar."

I jumped at the sound of this apparent mind reader. I had been alone on Norfolk Avenue. I was alone no longer.

There was more than one. In fact, I was surrounded by a crowd. The Gypsies had arrived.

CHAPTER 30 – SURROUNDED

Finally, my feelings of being watched and followed proved to have merit. This new knowledge was of little consolation. On the contrary, I felt nauseous. Those surrounding me did not look friendly.

In the crowd, I saw a few familiar faces. I recognized the fake nurse. She had a swollen, discolored eye and was still missing one of her fake eyelashes.

Beside her stood one with even more injury to his face. It surprised me to see the damage the hospital's stolen flashlight had been capable of inflicting.

I also recognized the two who had broken into Mrs. Scholes' home. That didn't surprise me, not now that I understood the scope of the gypsies' reach. With their organized crime connections, I was sure they had no problem hiring a crooked attorney who convinced a judge to allow for their release.

I looked at those break-in artists and felt anger welling up within me like lava inside a high-pressure volcano. These two ran free while Mrs. Scholes was confined to a hospital room! I was old enough to know how things worked. They were probably given a court date they were unlikely to show up for. Sure, warrants would be issued for them, but by then they'd be long gone, probably with new birth certificates and social security numbers.

I estimated maybe twenty-five people surrounded me. Given that moments ago, I had been on the deserted streets of late-night/early morning Norfolk, this crowd seemed every bit as substantial as those found in greater metropolitan areas during the noonday rush. Some in the crowd looked as young as me. Others were older. One woman looked as old as time itself.

Judging from the quality of the voice that had spoken of a crowbar, I guessed it was the old one who had spoken. In her hand she did indeed hold a crowbar. What really made me nervous was that she hefted it more like a weapon than a tool.

This woman, I noticed seemed to be the focal point of the scene. All the others seemed to wait on her, and I found I was no different.

She wasn't much to look at. As skinny as she was, she could have hidden behind a flagpole and not been spotted. Although as skinny as a flagpole, she wasn't as straight. Apparently, she hadn't gotten enough calcium in her youth.

I had never thought long hair on elderly women was an especially attractive fashion statement. That goes doubly true when that long hair is as tangled and unkempt as hers was.

She looked like the poster child for the SWG, the *Stereotypical Witch Guild*. I didn't know if such a group existed, but if it did, she would be a shoe-in.

What commanded my attention more than anything was that, in the hand that didn't hold the crowbar, she held my gun. The dangerous end was pointed at me!

I felt fear, laced with feelings of stupidity, rise inside me like an ominous cancer. The origins of the fear was obvious. The stupidity however came as a direct result of my own bad decisions. You would think that after leaving the Bible unattended back in room 119, I would have learned to keep the important things in my grasp at all times. Yet here I was, caught without my gun just when it would have come in handy.

I thought back to when I had set down the weapon. I had been so focused on getting the cover off the statue's base, I didn't think twice about what I had done. In retrospect, that was probably the cue to the gypsies to come out of hiding, what with me being unarmed and all. It was a rookie mistake on my part, no doubt.

I tried hard to find the positive side. Perhaps not having the gun in hand was a good thing. I was vastly outnumbered and even if I could shoot well (which I could not) and even if every bullet blew away one of the enemy (which would not have been likely), I would still have to fight off those that remained once my gun was empty.

This group looked as if they were used to fighting. I, on the other hand, was just a boy. My entire fighting career consisted of watching action films, after-school TV programs like Maverick, and my personal experiences of the last forty-eight hours.

Yes, I thought, *it was a good thing I didn't have my gun*. In the heat of the moment, who knew if I would have made a stupid decision and pulled the trigger?

CHAPTER 31 – REMOVE NOT THE ANCIENT LANDMARK

Remove not the ancient landmark which thy fathers have set. This proverb kept running over and over in my mind.

The business end of the gun pointed at my chest. The old woman stood no further away than a few feet away. If she fired, it would be point blank. I would be good for only one thing: pushing up daisies.

The old woman grinned at me, and it was not a pretty site. First of all, she was short some teeth. Secondly, the few she did have were dingy. Let's just say I don't think she had the luxury of dental insurance.

Her grin morphed into a chuckle, or more accurately, it morphed into a cackle that would have made any self-respecting hag envious. The rest joined in, as if they shared a collective consciousness. It wasn't pleasant laughter, at least not from my point of view.

"Thank you, boy," she said as the cackle died down to a mild guffaw. "All we wanted from you was the Bible, but you did us one better and brought us right to the treasure as well. Not too shabby for a boy with no gypsy blood, not too shabby at all."

I was having trouble paying attention to the old crackpot. My attention deficit problems were kicking in big time. Simply put, the gun had stolen my ability to concentrate on much else.

Its barrel bred fear in me. One slip of that gnarled trigger finger would mean instantly getting close and personal with Jesus. Although I was not opposed to entering heaven, I was opposed to going there at my age due to acute lead poisoning of the worst kind.

To a lesser extent, my brain still occupied itself with self-chastisement. Even though I had already determined it was a good thing I didn't have the gun in hand at a critical moment when I may have impulsively fired it, still it was a dumb mistake and one I was sure Magnum P.I. would never have made.

In addition to all of this, that proverb kept looping over and over through my head. *Remove NOT the ancient landmark which thy fathers have set.*

I looked up at the ancient landmark. He held his pint of beer high as if he were really enjoying himself, which made me a little angry. *How dare he be so happy when I was about to get a full-body bullet shower!*

Deep down, I knew it was ludicrous to be so annoyed at this lifeless sculpture. It was not capable of being happy or sad, or anything else for that matter. It was only an inanimate object, void of life or emotion. The statue's other hand, the one not holding the beer, pointed ominously to the space in front of the tavern's door of eyes, down at the concrete sidewalk.

The old lady was talking to me. I could see her lips moving, but with all the other things roaring through my brain, I really wasn't listening to her words. In my ears, she sounded like an adult from an old *Peanuts* cartoon, *waa waa waa waa waaaaah.*

I caught the occasional bit or piece. She was saying something about how gypsies were so very sly and how I was so very delusional for thinking I could outwit them.

Remove NOT the ancient landmark which thy fathers had set, my brain-waves overrode her voice. There was something important in that proverb, something I was missing. But what?

The old hag kept ranting on and on about who knows what. The gun remained pointed at me. The proverb kept looping through my brain like a record with a bad scratch.

My eyes followed the statue's pointing finger. It pointed just in front of the door of eyes. It was pointing at the inconsequential sidewalk.

Then it hit me. It was not just sidewalk. A manhole was there. Why would a manhole be there? I had never before seen a manhole on a sidewalk. To the best of my recollection, they were always found on the streets.

I looked back at the gun still directed at me. In my mental background I heard the droning of the woman's demented speech. I looked back at the out-of-place manhole.

Remove NOT the ancient landmark... Remove <u>NOT</u> the ancient landmark!

Suddenly, all of the puzzle pieces fell into place. I saw the big picture and my stomach did a serious flip.

CHAPTER 32 – THE MEANING OF THE PROVERB

I realized the meaning of the proverb and my heart jumped into my throat. Was I too late in discovering this meaning? I hoped not. Being too late would be fatal.

Remove NOT the ancient landmark which thy fathers have set. I watched in fear as the old woman handed the crowbar to one of the younger men.

That younger man had been holding a flashlight. He set it down, took the crowbar and began to pry at the edges of the plaque. They were doing exactly what I had tried to do with my quarter just a few moments ago. But that was then and this was now, and now I realized, they were doing exactly what the proverb was warning against!

The lid flipped off and clattered to the ground bottom side up. The whole crowd pushed forward no doubt expecting to lay greedy eyes upon the glorious treasure.

Their efforts to see were pointless. I now knew this. No treasure awaited them, at least not there. I saw the plaque land on the sidewalk. I caught the slightest glimpse before the gathering crowd blocked it from my sight, but that was all I needed to sound the alarms.

The statue was not the landmark. The plaque was. It had now been removed.

I recognized the four items connected to the lid. I had watched enough reruns of *Hogan's Heroes* and old John Wayne war movies. They were grenade pins!

I stumbled back through the tide of gypsies crowding in like a herd of hungry cattle at feeding time. It seemed I was the only one who had seen the danger.

I turned, desperately swimming against the tide. I stumbled and fell to the ground. I crawled through the forest of legs crowding in toward the coming calamity.

I didn't know how much time I had. According to all the old war movies I had seen on TV, it was only seconds. Those seconds ticked by like an eternity. I pushed out beyond the masses and struggled back to my feet. Then I ran like there was no tomorrow!

I tried to serpentine as best I could, thinking bullets would whiz by at any second, but no shots were fired. At the moment, I was inconsequential to them. The hoped-for treasure had their complete attention.

I sprinted across the vacant street as fast as I could, seeking cover. Unfortunately, there were no ancient landmarks on this side of Norfolk Avenue that I could hide behind. There was only a postal service drop-off mailbox. I dove behind it, hoping the U.S. Postal Service reinforced their blue bins.

For a moment, I wondered if fifty-year-old grenades were still live. I wondered for only a moment. Then, I knew. They were definitely still live.

The boom was deafening. The blast rocked me backwards. The mailbox vibrated, but luckily for me, it was bolted to the sidewalk and held its position.

Bits of shrapnel flew like miniature rockets. Some pinged the mailbox. Some whizzed past me at speeds that made them a blur. I nearly blacked out from terror.

The windows in the storefronts behind me shattered into a plethora of glittery shards. Strangely enough, my first thought was *man, those store owners are going to be ticked-off tomorrow when they come to work.*

What a strange thought, given the situation. Then again, how would I know if it was strange? I had never been in such a situation before. Maybe such thoughts were as right as rain in such circumstances.

A bronze hand holding a pint of beer landed just to my right, creating a chipped crater into the street's curb. It rattled to a rest and moved no more.

The boom died off and all that was left was a constant ringing I assumed only I could hear. I hoped the ringing would die soon. I certainly didn't want permanent hearing loss.

I peeked out from my hiding place. I spied the devastation. I ran back to the crime scene.

I had much to do and had little time to do it. The police would be here any moment. I couldn't afford to be detained.

CHAPTER 33 – INTO DARKNESS

I acted on a hunch and was proud to do so. After all, hunch-acting was very Magnum P.I.

In the distance, I could hear sirens blaring. The authorities were on their way. I couldn't afford to be delayed, not for a moment because who knew how many enemies were still around that were too powerful for Norfolk police protection capabilities?

I glanced up and down Norfolk Avenue. With the exception of the recently deceased, it was deserted. Luckily for me, there was no residential housing along this street which gave me a smidgeon of confidence that no witnesses were yet watching my movements. At least that was my hope.

Soon, very soon, the street would be filled with police, paramedics, and every slack-jawed local who lived within earshot of the recent blast. I didn't need that kind of publicity.

As fast as I could, I ran to where the statue had been. Ground zero. What a mess.

Guts everywhere: this verified that although Mrs. Scholes portrayed them as evil demons, they were only human and substantially less than immortal. I couldn't help but feel both sadness and repulsion at the sight. Now however, there was no time to mourn or gag.

I didn't see the Gypsy leader, but judging by my memory of her frail frame, she had probably vaporized into nothingness in the explosion.

None of the bodies moved as I tip-toed around them. I was sure they had traveled beyond the realm of the living. The creep-out factor was substantial as I moved among them. At any moment, I half-expected a bloody zombie-like hand to claw out at me and demand my brains for their dinner.

Again, I was acting on a hunch. I ran to the door of eyes—the last known location of the old lady.

The door had held, although many of the eyes were now chipped, marred, and flecked with blood. The stained glass windows didn't fare as well. Not one piece of glass remained. The manhole that had lain directly before the door of eyes was in-tact. I stared at it. It was weird to have a manhole on the sidewalk in front of a storefront property. The ancient landmark had pointed directly to that spot. And lastly, there was the plaque. *I welcome those free of the Gypsy curse. Those not under the curse may enter through the door and enjoy the treasure of the Evil Eye.*

My hunch was starting to coalesce. The ancient landmark, I conjectured, was not where the treasure was. *Remove not the ancient landmark.* Those words of warning now made sense.

Those not under the curse may enter through the door and enjoy the treasure of the Evil Eye. The statue had not pointed to the door of eyes. It had pointed to the out-of-place manhole. I looked at the cover more closely. It did not say *City of Norfolk* like all the others in town. It had no label whatsoever.

All this thinking took place in seconds. The sirens were growing louder. The law was drawing nearer. I looked down the street. No one had arrived yet, but I could see the flashing red and blues that showed the authorities were just around the bend.

Without a second thought. I grabbed the crowbar from the corpse that still held it. It didn't come easily from his death grip, but I was in way too deep to give up now. I pulled hard and ripped it free. Then, I quickly went to work with the tool and opened the door, not the door of eyes, but the secret door to which all hints pointed.

For some reason, I expected the light from the streetlamps to reveal a golden glow of treasure, but I was sorely disappointed. I saw only darkness. The light didn't penetrate more than a few feet down. The sirens were louder than ever. I did what I had to do.

I grabbed the flashlight which the younger gypsy had put down and which miraculously appeared undamaged by the blast. Then I descended.

An iron-rung ladder was attached to the side of the hole, making my descent possible. It groaned in protest under my weight and I could feel rust-crumbles flaking off in my hands as I gripped it. It was clear nobody had been on that ladder in years, possibly decades. I used it nonetheless as it was all there was.

Now only my head was above street level. I took in a final glance. No signs of life presented themselves. A slight breeze picked up. A few pages from a pulverized bible blew past. Oh well, I guess it had served its purpose. Still, it was sad to see my book of salvation was no more.

After I had gone down past my head level, I held my breath, said a prayer, and flicked the switch on the flashlight. My prayer was answered. It worked.

Momentarily, I looked up at the circle of stars shining down into my hole. I resisted my feelings of claustrophobia and fought the urge to re-ascend back to the street. Instead, I reached up and pulled the manhole over the opening.

The lid fell into place with a sound of finality. Despite the feeling I had just buried myself alive, my escape was now complete.

CHAPTER 34 - DOWN

Into the gloom I continued to descend. The ladder was precarious. I descended with caution, a spider on the thinnest of gossamer threads. Every step I took brought me deeper down and further from the chaos one world up. And every step that increased that distance, increased my thankfulness.

My flashlight cut a swath of light down the vertical shaft as I descended further and further. To my frustration, it revealed no treasure. It showed only damp spaces that had been in perpetual darkness for who knows how long.

As I thought about the treasure I was going after and those who had tried to beat me to it, I suddenly remembered scripture from a recent Sunday morning sermon. I was uncertain why I thought of such seemingly inconsequential things at that moment. Perhaps this new sensory deprivation environment encouraged my thoughts to wander and remember the sermon. It had been entitled: *Money is the root of all kinds of evil.* How true I now knew this to be.

Regardless of all the evil that had befallen me as a result of this treasure, I kept pursuing it. It was evil money to be sure, obtained through coercion and ill-gotten tactics. Still, I had to keep after it. Giving up risked life itself.

I needed it to save myself and Mrs. Scholes from the hands of the Tabitha's—if any of them still lived. And even if none did, there was still the larger crime organizations they were connected with and who no doubt had their stakes in the claim. Certainly, those less-than-moral syndicates would need to be appeased with this blood money even if Tabitha's band themselves were permanently out of the picture.

Another saying came to mind, one not stated in the Sunday-morning sermons, but true nonetheless. *Money is power.* So, here I was running after evil power money and desperately hoping it wouldn't end badly.

My foot splashed into water. I had reached the bottom. The water wasn't deep. My socks didn't even get wet as the water didn't rise above the rubber soles of my shoes.

The sloshing of my feet, as they broke the dark, wet surface, echoed through the chamber I now found myself in. It was unsettling, to say the least. I stood absolutely still as the lapping at my feet dissipated and the echoes of my intrusion bounded back and forth, weaker with every revolution until they were no more.

My only security rested with the weapon I held. *Oh crap.* My weapon wasn't in my hand. I must have left the crowbar up on the street, probably setting it down to grab the flashlight. Such were the actions of one afflicted with attention deficit problems.

I thought I heard another noise as my splashy echoes died away. I couldn't be sure but I thought it came from above. I pointed the flashlight up the ladder, but the beam didn't penetrate all the way up, just as it had not revealed this watery world when I had pointed it down from on high.

The last of the echoes from my landing faded into oblivion. Only silence remained.

I stood there staring up the ladder. The beam of light revealed nothing.

No further sounds traveled down to my ears. Unfortunately, the ringing in my ears, although less intense than it had been right after the blast, persisted. So, my hearing was not up to par, which made me doubt my senses.

This new realm in which I existed was disorienting. I conjectured it was possible the sounds I thought I heard were nothing more than a combination of the echoes of my own feet and the silent shrieks of my overstimulated imagination. After all, this had not been an everyday, run of the mill night and my brain had been pushed to the verge of maximum overload.

In light of my reduced-hearing ability, I tried to compensate with other senses. I stared up at the ladder, squinting my eyes in hopes of seeing more. I saw nothing. I tried to sense a change in air pressure against my skin, but nada. I even tried to conjure up some hidden sixth sense. Again, nothing.

I couldn't afford to freeze up, not now, not after getting this far. I had to push on, past my many barriers of fear. Reluctantly, I redirected my flashlight beam from where I had just been, to where I needed to go.

The tunnel I faced housed a whole new mess of fears. It was damp and dark. I imagined it to be the open throat of a giant snake, ready to invite me in to consume me whole.

Regardless of these inhibiting thoughts, I had no choice. It was the only way unless I decided to chicken out and go back up the ladder. But going back up meant exposure to the police who had no doubt swarmed the area by now. Worse, what if I bumped into that which I may or may not have heard and may or may not exist outside of my imagination? I moved on.

The tunnel was concrete and perfectly round. It angled slightly downhill. The sides were stained, no doubt by alternating periods of wet and dry. I walked on. A small but steady trickle of water rushed down the decline, along my feet.

The tunnel was only about four and a half feet in diameter which required me to hunch over as I went along so I had plenty of opportunity to observe the trickling water. It was no doubt a result of the earlier storm, making me wonder if the tunnel was connected to the city's main water drainage system. I walked on.

I had the urge to look back. The feeling of being watched and followed had grown ever since I'd heard the sounds above in the first chamber of this subterranean world.

I dared not turn, knowing that if I did, I would have to confront whatever lurked there. The gypsies were back there on Norfolk Avenue in front of the blast-damaged door of eyes, dead as dead could be. But much more sinister things lurked in such places as I now traveled; at least that was what any number of horror flicks had taught me over the years.

It took effort, but I kept my flashlight trained on the dark tunnel ahead. If my hunch was right and it connected to the city's drainage system, then it should eventually empty into the Elkhorn. In that case, I would need to stay vigilant in my approach. In this darkness, unless I kept my flashlight shining ahead of me, I might take one too many steps and suddenly find myself plummeting headfirst into the river. That was something I didn't want to do.

After such a storm as had just blown through town, the river would be swift and swollen. I was not a strong swimmer. In fact, I often struggled to keep my head above water in swimming pools so I guessed a river at flood-stage would be above my ability to survive.

I had no idea how far from the river I was. The tunnel was disorienting in that way. I continued.

And then—I froze. Again, I thought I heard noises. I couldn't tell for sure. If they existed, they stopped the second I did. Silence reigned.

In the tunnel, I couldn't tell if the noise I thought I heard had come from in front of me, or behind. I held my breath, and stood perfectly still, poised to break into a run at any moment. I listened with all my might, pushing past the incessant ringing in my ears, but failed to pick up any sound beyond the gurgle of the trickling waters at my feet and the unusually loud *lub-dub* of my pounding heart.

I tried to push the fear away, telling myself the sounds were imaginary. I was alone. I had to be, right? I mean, everyone up there on the street had died in the blast. I was the lone survivor.

Regardless of how hard I tried to convince myself, the feeling I was in the presence of unwanted company persisted, festered, and grew by the second like a malicious parasite.

My fears escalated further as my flashlight beam began to flicker like a strobe light. At first, I was confused. The only reason I could think of was that my batteries were wearing down. Until then, I hadn't thought what would happen if my light went out. Now I thought of it and cowered in my terror.

But after a moment, realization dawned and relief flooded me. Dead batteries was not the problem. My hand was shaking so badly that the light was vibrating with my shivers.

I gripped the flashlight with both hands to steady myself and wished I still had a weapon. I had left the gun above on Norfolk Avenue, probably in the cold, dead clutches of the one who had taken it from me, and of course there was the crowbar I exchanged up there for the flashlight.

In truth, guns and crowbars would be of little use if the creatures my mind was conjuring were really following me. In my imagination, I saw the bony fingers of a sewer zombie, slowly emerging from the darkness to throttle my neck and eat my brains.

Finally, I could take it no more. In a panic, I spun.

I stared into the portion of tunnel I had recently traveled. As far as the beam penetrated, no sewer zombies, or giant alligators, or demons from hell, or any other of my imagined dangers were coming at me. As far as I could tell, I was alone. I was very alone.

But who knew what lurked beyond the range of my beam. This thought reinvigorated my imagination. In my mind's eye, I still saw all the creatures I've already mentioned plus a few new ones too grotesque to describe. I was almost certain said creatures were hiding just beyond the light's reach.

Quickly, I took a step in that direction, extending the range of vision by the distance of that step. I flinched as I stepped forward, fully expecting a beast to suddenly appear in the light, but nothing did. Nothing emerged into my view other than what was known to be there; just tunnel, water, and empty space. Still, I knew that farther back, beyond the light there was a plethora of hiding places; enough room for an entire army of Hell's creatures.

I turned and continued along the tunnel, quicker than before. I was acutely aware of the similarities between where I was headed and Alice's famous journey down the rabbit hole that led to Wonderland. *Off with his head!* A voice deep down inside of me erupted. *Off with his head!* I shivered with renewed terror.

My feet moved quicker by the moment as I lumbered further down the tunnel, trying hard to keep my head from banging into the low ceiling. I now looked more like a hunchback running a marathon than the boy I was. Under other circumstances, such a marathon would have been comical, but these were not other circumstances. This was, to put it bluntly, my living nightmare.

CHAPTER 35 – ALONE?

Honestly, I wasn't sure where I was going. The last time I felt any sense of direction was from the pointing finger of the ancient landmark. Since then, I'd been going on sheer instinct. Could I trust my instinct? I was hopeful, but not confident.

Although I wasn't sure where I was going, I was far from lost. The tunnel had not yet branched off into other passageways. So, I continued in the only direction available.

I worried what I would do if the tunnel did branch off. I suspected this would occur eventually, especially if the tunnel was connected to the city system. What would I do then?

I supposed I would cross that bridge when I got to it. In the meantime, I made an effort to push the self-defeating thoughts from my mind. I could ill afford such worries. For one thing, worrying would do nothing to improve my situation. Secondly, I had far more pressing matters at hand that demanded my attention.

For example, I still had the unsettling feeling I was being stalked. I had nothing solid to base this feeling on other than sounds which may have been imaginary or real—I could not yet decide. All I knew was that my intuition was tingling and I did not like it one bit.

My mind continued to conjure up creatures that might live in such places as the city drainage system. I imagined such creatures would likely relish unsuspecting kids like me for a snack. Again, I tried to push such thoughts away, a thing more easily said than done.

You could call my suspicions a gut reaction. Plus, despite the ringing in my ears, I could hear the occasional soft movement behind me. Nothing loud or particularly threatening, just scuffling sounds that betrayed the one who was following.

That's when I decided to stop kidding myself. The sounds were not imaginary, but real.

I stopped again and listened. As before, the sounds stopped as I did. I tried to recant the fact that I had just determined those sounds were real. I tried to tell myself it was still possible these suspicious noises were my own and it only appeared to be coming from behind me because of the crazy acoustics in the tunnel. I tried hard to convince myself of this, but ultimately this sales pitch to myself fell flat. I knew the truth and although it frightened me greatly, I couldn't deny it.

I began to walk, and again I swore I heard the unseen follower start up behind me. Whatever it was, it possessed intelligence. The follower knew enough to be quiet when I was and to move when I did.

I stopped, spun quickly and nearly lost my balance. I staggered for a moment, using the tunnel for support. I directed my light toward the noise, hoping to expose the creeper.

I exposed nothing.

This further reinforced my theory. Whatever was behind me was smart enough to stay beyond the reach of my flashlight and to anticipate my every move.

"I know you're there!" I called out as I gave up trying to convince myself I was alone. "I know you're following me!"

The sound of my voice was alarming. I was trying with all of my might to sound tough. I was failing. I sounded frightened and vulnerable and those are two traits one never wants to portray when being stalked in a dark tunnel by an unseen, presumably evil creature.

I stood for a second or two and waited for a response, any response, but nothing came back to me. Only silence. The intense quiet of the situation was deafening. I had almost hoped something would respond. At least that would have brought hidden secrets out into the open. At least I would have known what I was confronting.

It was quiet, too quiet. If the situation had not been so serious, I would have chuckled at my mind's conjuring of this overused movie cliché. However, the situation *was* more than quiet. It was serious, deadly serious.

I was alone with the exception of this unseen creeper. I felt like shrieking for help, but no one would hear me down in this rat-hole, except the one who was following me.

With effort, I kept my screams bottled inside. I didn't want the creeper to witness this further weakness on my part and resolved I would not give him/her/it that satisfaction.

Screaming or silent, one thought permeated my brain. Something was out there and it was biding its time, waiting for me to let my guard down, waiting for me to peter out. I couldn't afford to give it an opportunity to strike. I turned forward and bolted down the tunnel, full speed ahead.

My imagination became my worst enemy, conjuring wicked thoughts of what might be tailing me as I fled. I imagined tribes of gypsies, all dead from the grenade explosion, now animated by some dark magic. I imagined them coming for me, preparing to force me to join their legion of the damned.

As I ran, the flashlight beam bounced wildly about. This only added to the macabre feel of the situation. In my head, Michael Jackson's *Thriller* began to play. In the darkest regions of my imagination, the dead gypsies came out and began to dance in choreographed movements, just like in the music video. In my mind, I tried to escape them, but despite my best efforts, they danced ever nearer.

Fear propelled me down the tunnel as fuel does a rocket. One priority superseded all the rest. I had to put as much distance as possible between myself and the evil things behind me.

Suddenly the thought coalesced that maybe the evil things that pursued me *wanted* me to go this way. Maybe they were coaxing me into a trap. I remembered learning in school about how some prehistoric tribes used a tactic where they would stampede herds of bison toward a cliff and drive them off of the edge to kill them for food. Maybe I was their bison. Maybe I was their food!

I shuddered at that thought and planted myself. My feet slid on the slippery wet tunnel floor before I came to a stop. I stared into the tunnel ahead of me. Then I spun again to confront whatever had been herding me forward. "What do you want?" I shrieked.

No answer.

I let out a war cry, or at least an attempt at a war cry. It sounded more fearful than brave, more kitten than lion.

No answer.

I spun and continued to run from that which I was sure was hot on my heels. Just as one feels the wind without seeing it, so it was at that moment. I couldn't see the one who hunted me, but I could feel its haunting presence. I knew it was out there, and that knowledge spurred me ever closer to the precipice of madness.

In my deranged state, I had forgotten that this tunnel was likely to empty at some point into the Elkhorn. I remembered it suddenly, but it was too late. The tunnel ended.

CHAPTER 36 – END OF THE LINE

Caught off guard, I dropped my flashlight. It fell ten feet before splashing into the Elkhorn and disappearing into the river's dark depths. This would have bothered me more if I hadn't had other, more important things to deal with—like the fact I was at risk for following suit.

I grasped at the wet smooth sides of the tunnel just before it ended, but the slick walls provided nothing for me. Luckily, my reflexes kicked in at the last possible fraction of a second. I found a steel support beam that ran along the top and marked the end of the tunnel. Thank goodness for modern building code.

I gripped the beam with all my strength, but my fingers were so sweaty and the beam was so wet. My hands were slipping, but I couldn't allow myself to let go. My body flew out with the momentum of my flight. My legs swung out over the river like a pendulum. My fingers slid until only the last joint on four fingers, two on each hand, held me to the beam. That was all that stood between me and a watery grave—four straining fingers.

The eternity I experienced as I dangled over the Elkhorn was in reality, no more than a second. The pendulum that was me, reversed itself and I landed back in the tunnel in an uncoordinated dance. My arms felt as if they had been ripped from their sockets and my fingers burned.

I dropped to my knees, trying to catch my breath. My body shivered with fright and I realized at that moment I was definitely not Thomas Magnum caliber. I was more like Shaggy from Scooby-Doo.

I looked over my shoulder, staring into the darkness to the flood-enraged river. I held out my hand toward the waters, but nothing happened. No matter how much I wished, no matter how hard I concentrated, the flashlight wouldn't listen to my Jedi mind-powers. I guess I wasn't Luke Skywalker any more than I was Magnum.

There was something strange about what had just happened. Of course nearly plummeting out of a drainage tunnel into the Elkhorn River in the middle of the night was in itself a bit outside of the scope of my ordinary schedule, but there was something more. I couldn't quite put my finger on it.

I stared back into the darkness of the tunnel through which I had so recently careened. My little acrobatic act had momentarily taken my focus from the monsters I was sure lurked in that tunnel, but now that my act was done, my fears returned for the encore.

Something lurked back there in the darkness, hiding and waiting. Whatever it was, I was more vulnerable to it than ever, without my flashlight.

I tried to will my eyes into suddenly obtaining night vision, but the darkness was intense and my eyes remained nothing more or less than human. Apparently, I had no more the ability to exchange my eyes for those of a cat's, then I did power to become a Jedi master and retrieve my flashlight from the river.

I saw shapes coming toward me from the darkness, but I couldn't tell if they were real or imagined. Nothing grabbed me except my terror, so I suppose that was a good thing, depending on your point of view.

Still, I knew something was out there, something real, and it was biding its time, waiting for the best moment to pounce upon its prey. I strained my ears and swore I heard unsavory sounds travel to me from down that tunnel. I wondered if they were, like the shapes, nothing but a manifestation of my terror. I hoped they were. I feared otherwise. Zombies, vampires, werewolves, mutant alligators—they were all following me in my mind's eye.

A bump echoed from the darkness. I knew for sure this time that it was not my imagination. That was the moment my terror-meter flew off the charts. My eyes widened to the point of aching. I had to see, I needed to see, but the darkness was so overwhelming, so complete.

Another noise, like the first came to me. Whatever made the sound was closer than it had been just moments before.

I felt behind me and found the end of the tunnel. From below came the rushing of the Elkhorn. There was no escape that way.

In my panic, my thoughts went back to when I had almost fallen into the river. Only the support beam, four fingers, and my determination had saved me. A memory rushed to the front of my mind. In the brief moment I had been dangling, I had noticed something—something that was significant somehow, yet I couldn't quite put my finger on it.

Something had been out of place out, something I barely glimpsed as my flashlight flew into the river. What was it? *Think, man.*

I looked out into the night beyond the end of the tunnel, but only darkness marginally less complete than inside the tunnel greeted me. What was I trying to remember? *Think-think-think*!

I turned back towards the tunnel once again. Another of those noises came to me, closer still. "Who's there?" I squeaked.

Just as before, no answer came back but the echo of my own voice. By this time, the hidden lurker was not fooling me in the least. I knew of its existence and this knowledge was pushing me to the outskirts of Crazy town.

Light! It suddenly hit me. *I had seen light!*

That's what had been out there that should not have been. Everything was dark. It was night. Yet, a light had been outside the tunnel.

"Silly child."

The voice made me jump. I had waited so long for solid proof of the one who followed me. Now I had proof, I wished I didn't.

A match was struck, a corncob pipe was lit and a face flared out of the darkness. I gasped and stepped back as far as I could without falling down into the churning waters of the rain-gorged river.

The lips that held the pipe grinned as it drew in the smoke so that the match that was being held to the tobacco flared brightly with every puff. I knew this face—but it was impossible! I *saw* the explosion on Norfolk Avenue. I saw the dead tribe with my own eyes. They had all been blown to smithereens!

"Where is my treasure, silly boy?" she asked with bitterness in her voice.

The old hag had seen better days. When last we met, up on the street, she had been ugly and old. Now, with her grenade-shrapnel injuries, she looked even worse.

A deep gash had torn her face open from her left cheek down to the bottom of her chin. It exposed her teeth all the way to her ear so that she looked like a grinning corpse. It amazed me she could make the pipe work at all, but somehow she managed.

She glared at me with one angry yellow eye. The other squinted shut with bloody tears dripping from it.

She no longer had my gun, at least as far as I could see. Perhaps it had been damaged in the blast. Instead, she held a knife, the sort Sylvester Stallone always held when he was being John Rambo. She held it with surprising steadiness, given her condition. I had no doubt she could carve me up quicker than a Thanksgiving turkey.

"I'm not going to ask you a second time, boy. Where is my treasure?" She waved the blade wildly in front of her. By the light of her pipe, she looked positively demonic. Plus, her injuries lent well to the whole legion of the undead vibe. It was a miracle she had survived at all. It was a dreadfully unfortunate miracle.

She seemed able to read my thoughts. "It's a good thing I saw the booby trap for what it was. I had just enough time to use the young man next to me as a shield. Too bad for him. Of course it's a dog eat dog world. Better him than me."

She chuckled. The chuckle morphed into spasms of coughing. She was not in good shape.

My only hope now was the knowledge of the light where no light should have been. I had to act on a hunch and I hoped to God that that hunch was correct.

With a scream of fury, she let her corncob pipe fall to the ground where it momentarily lit the tunnel with a splash of tobacco-sparks. Simultaneously, she lunged at me.

That knife cleaved the air. It would have cleaved me as well, but I acted just a split second quicker than she did.

I took a leap of faith—a very literal leap. I jumped from the tunnel.

CHAPTER 37 – A HOLLOW SPACE

I heard cursing and other assorted expletives as I swung out into the darkness, gripping the support beam for dear life, making sure this time my fingers didn't slip. She must have been shouting with all her might because I could hear her cursing even over the rush of the mighty Elkhorn surging just below me.

Dangling over the river, directly in front of the tunnel opening, I was a sitting duck. In the dark I couldn't see her, but I knew this devil-woman was coming for me with knife in hand and murder in heart.

With no time to lose, I swung to the right, to where I had seen the light.

The eerie glow still emanated there. On the convex side of the concrete drainage pipe tunnel I had just left, there was a hollow space. It wasn't much, less than two feet in width, no more than a crack where the earth had eroded away between the tunnel and an ancient exposed section of tree root.

It was such an insignificant anomaly that I would never have seen it if that light hadn't been shining out from it. I swung into the hole just as the old lady's blade flashed out at me, glimmering in the dimness.

I tried to dodge her. I failed.

A burning sensation overwhelmed my thigh. I shrieked out in fear and pain. I could hear the old gypsy hag cackle at my scream. Apparently, my pain was her joy.

I wiggled into the hollow space like a night crawler escaping a hungry robin. One wound was more than enough for me; in fact, I questioned my ability to survive a second.

The light, although it shone out brightly in contrast to the surrounding darkness, was actually quite dim. I tried to get a good look at my leg, but I couldn't see enough to determine if it was a serious injury, a mere nick, or something in between.

It stung like the dickens, as Mrs. Scholes would say in such a situation. I reached down to touch it. I felt the warm stickiness of blood. It didn't seem to be spurting from the wound, which was good, and I suspected I would live.

"Get back here, boy!" I heard her raspy voice outside the cave. "You can't get away from me!"

Well, my mom and dad didn't raise no fool, and I most certainly did not comply with her demand. Instead, I slid further into the cave and in so doing, slid further in towards the light.

This new tunnel was deeper than it led on to be by the humble appearance of its entrance. The further in I wiggled, the brighter the light grew and the more spacious my surroundings became.

In this new, better light, I looked at my palm, the one that had put pressure on my thigh. It was red with blood. I knew it was my blood and the sight of it made me queasy.

I overrode my pansy ways and forced myself to look again at the wound. It appeared to have stopped bleeding for the most part and didn't seem as bad as I had feared. Still, it hurt and using the injured leg was more difficult than it had been before the stabbing.

I looked about me. Despite the recent deluge, the cave was relatively dry. I squirmed farther in, my wet body leaving a damp trail like the slime of a retreating slug.

After a few more feet, the cave widened. Here the light was the brightest. I scanned the room in which I found myself, in shock. I had found the treasure!

CHAPTER 38 – ALL THINGS GLITTERY

The room was filled with all things glittery. Most of it appeared to be gold and silver coinage.

I picked up one of the coins and stared at it in awe. Above my head, was a single bare bulb dangling by a free-hanging wire. The bulb swayed minutely on the wire, giving the room an eerie macabre feel. It was by this light that I read the year of the coin's minting. I was holding a 1935 silver dollar.

I looked about. Most of the treasure sat in old-looking wooden crates, but a few potato sacks also dotted the landscape.

One of the nearer crates advertised coke for a nickel. Another advertised some sort of chewing gum made from cloves. A third was labeled *Horehound Candy.*

I had no idea what horehound was, but was fairly certain such an ingredient had no right being in candy to begin with. It sounded more like a label fitting of Jake the infamous Devil-dog from my past.

The contents of some of the crates and bags spilled out through places that had weakened over time. Others held their wares, but strained under the pressure.

I turned the old coin over in my hand and let the light play on its shining surface. Suddenly, a thought entered my mind. *Who had turned on the light?*

I looked up at the bare bulb as it moved to the vibrations of the nearby rushing river and wondered if it could have possibly been left on since 1935? *Not likely*, I responded to myself.

Then a frightful question entered my mind. *Was that old hag following me in here?* The sight of the treasure had momentarily taken my focus away from this more pressing issue.

I tried to imagine her hanging over the river by the support beam with her Rambo knife clenched between her teeth. She was a crazy old biddy. That had been established. Now I wondered if she was crazy enough to follow me in here. I couldn't see how she could physically do it, given her age and injuries. Then again, insanity and determination have been known to breed a strength all their own. She was definitely *coo-coo for Cocoa puffs* and more determined than a starving dog chasing an open-backed meat wagon. Already she had survived a grenade blast and trailed me into the underground. *Why would she stop now?* As soon as that question escaped my brain, I knew the answer, *she wouldn't.*

With a start, I realized the gravity of my predicament. Frantically, I looked around for another exit. I found none. I was trapped.

"Get your filthy hands off of my beautiful treasure before you taint it!" I heard her raspy voice call out behind me.

I turned. There she was, knife in hand and as feisty as ever.

I dropped the coin. It rolled to her feet as if under the influence of some dark gypsy magic. It came to rest against the toe of her foot, a lean of affection.

"Boy," she said as blood-infused spit particles shot from her cheek-wound in a fine pink and frothy mist. "You have been a real thorn in my back side and that's a fact."

By the looks of her, I had been more than a thorn. The journey from the tunnel into this hole had further deteriorated her condition. Her whole body seemed to quiver as if it were about to evaporate out of sheer exhaustion. This observation might have calmed me if it weren't for the fact she still held that knife.

She took one gimpy step towards me, stumbling and staggering. For a moment, I thought she was going down. But then she steadied herself.

Darn, I thought as I took one step away.

She glared at me with her good eye. It was a glare I'll never forget.

"You can have the treasure," I said. "It's all yours."

"Don't you tell me things I already know. Don't you act like you're giving me some kind of handout, like I'm some sort of charity case."

I wasn't sure how to answer or even if I should. The knife had my attention as it swayed like a charmed cobra getting ready to strike.

"You're damn right it's mine," she added. "Every last bit of it."

"Just leave Mrs. Scholes and myself alone," I said. That was the whole reason I was here in the first place, to get leverage for our safety.

She huffed. "Where do you come off acting like you're giving me what was mine to begin with? Just take a whiff, this whole treasure smells of gypsies."

Again, I found myself at a loss as to how to respond. First of all, I didn't understand 'crazy,' and this lady was speaking it fluently. *What did that even mean?* I had no idea what the smell of gypsies even meant.

Secondly, it appeared my quest for the treasure meant nothing. Apparently, I had nothing to barter with and that royally sucked after all I'd been though to get it.

"It was never rightfully gypsy treasure," a gruff new voice boomed.

The old woman's one good eye popped wide with shock. She spun around to look at the newcomer.

I thought momentarily about using this sudden distraction to escape, but then I thought better of it. For one thing, the newcomer was blocking the only exit I knew of. Secondly, I would have to run past the woman and she still had the knife. Lastly, I had searched for the treasure so I could barter protection for myself and Mrs. Scholes. With this new development, I clung to a last strand of hope there was still some value there.

If the old gypsy seemed stunned to discover we were not alone, I was doubly so. I tried to see who it was, but the old woman blocked my view for the most part.

I felt like I knew this newcomer. His voice was familiar somehow, yet his identity eluded me.

"Who are you?" the old lady shrieked.

I could tell she was frustrated with this new and unanticipated interruption. From the anger in her voice, I guessed he didn't smell like a gypsy to her.

"Tabitha," the man said. "After all these years, you don't recognize me?"

I was in shock. This was Tabitha? *The* Tabitha? The beautiful woman Milo couldn't resist? *Man*, I thought. *Somebody had been beating her really hard with the ugly stick for a very long time. Either that or Milo had pretty low standards.*

"How do you know me?" she asked. Her voice was suddenly calm, completely out of character based on my experience with her so far.

"You really don't remember me?"

I sensed the newcomer had stepped further into the room because Tabitha suddenly tensed and gripped her knife as if ready to strike. I tensed, too, ready to fight or evade as the need arose.

The newcomer's identity remained a mystery. I tried hard to look around Tabitha to get a look at him, but like an artist putting things in perspective for the viewer, the closer gypsy was larger in the foreground than the newcomer beyond her.

"Tabitha." The man spoke calmly, but sternly. "Put down the knife and think into your past."

I couldn't see old Tabitha's face, but from behind, I saw her head hunched a bit and I could imagine her one good eye narrowing in thought.

Then she let out a rattling gasp. Either she was dying or the spark of recognition had ignited in her old brain. Personally, I was hoping for the former.

I sensed she was about to say something, but all that came out was another gasp. I swore she was going to hyperventilate and simultaneously have a heart attack about this guy, which would not necessarily be a bad thing.

"*No!*" she finally managed.

"Oh yes," the man replied. "It's good to see your memory isn't gone completely."

"It can't be you!" she said, with little more than a whisper.

She had grown nervous. She began to shift her weight from one foot to the other, as if she had to pee. Unfortunately, she didn't have to pee bad enough to drop the knife.

"Oh," the man said with a soft chuckle. "It most certainly can be me. In fact, I promise you that it most certainly *is* me."

"No! I know who you are. You're his ghost. Why are you haunting me?"

The man laughed. "*Boo!*"

She twitched as he said it and took a step backwards in my direction. Her hand which held the knife was trembling.

With these new developments, her focus seemed to devolve. I seemed to be totally forgotten. Still, I dared not try to escape. It was too risky.

"You're dead!" she hissed at the newcomer as if being alive was a sin.

"I'm afraid not, Tabitha." His voice was driving me crazy. It was so familiar, as if I had heard it somewhere, but maybe not in real life. Could he be somebody from a dream? Or maybe a character from a movie or TV show had somehow materialized into the real world to rescue me from this crazy old hag?

"Put down the knife, Tabitha." His voice was more serious now.

Her hand shook, but she didn't put down the knife. "This treasure is for us gypsies."

"How so?" the man asked coldly. There was no longer even a hint of chuckle in his voice. "Gypsy treasure? For God's sake, you're the only one left!"

"Regardless," she shouted in rage, "it's mine!"

"You stole it!" the newcomer retorted.

With a snort, she fired back, "That's the way we've always operated. That's the way we always had to operate. It was survival. We alone were bold enough to take what we wanted. Therefore, we are entitled to it."

"It doesn't have to be like that any longer, Tabitha. Anyone can change, even an old gal like you," he said.

She scoffed. "No. Stealing's more than survival. It's our life, a code we live by."

"Again, there is no 'we.' You're the only one left!" he said in exasperation.

"Then it's the code we die by, and I will honor their deaths by holding fast."

"Please, Tabitha. This is your last chance to make a right decision."

For a moment, I thought this last statement had pushed old Tabitha against the mental ropes. She didn't respond and her twitchy knife-hand suddenly became rock-steady. Perhaps she was preparing to surrender.

"There can be another way," the man added, chipping away at her defenses.

"You cared for me once upon a time," she said with a quivery voice.

The man said nothing. I could feel the tension in the space between them as it surged and pulsed. It was as thick as peanut butter, to quote Yukon Cornelius from *Rudolf the Red-nosed Reindeer*.

"We could have that again," she continued.

"Don't you think that ship sailed a long time ago?" he asked after a pause. He suddenly sounded calmer.

"On the contrary. I think your ship has finally come in."

"You're mistaken, Tabitha."

His voice was driving me crazy. Where had I heard it before? There was something in its tone, a quality that I could not pin down.

"Am I?" She took a step toward him. Her knife hand had become less tense. "Come on, sweetie. You're lonely, just like you were back when we first met. I see it in your eyes."

"No," he answered. And it sounded like he meant it although his voice didn't sound as authoritative as it had at the beginning. I hoped he meant it.

"You remember when we met, don't you? I know you do."

"Stop it, Tabitha."

"You know, there's more than enough treasure for both of us. You said it yourself, I'm the only one left. We could share, what do you say?"

"Don't come a step closer, Tabitha." His voice took on a hint of pleading.

"I know it must have taken a long time to get over me. But now you can have it all again."

"Stop," the man whined.

"I'm sorry, sweetie. I really loved you. It was the others. They made me do it. I had no choice."

This time the stranger remained silent. This worried me.

"I had no choice," she wheedled. "They were family, and family sticks together."

The newcomer let out a moan that bordered on a sob.

"But now they're dead. There's no family left. It's just you and me."

"What about him? What about the boy behind you?"

Why? Why did you have to remind her about me? I flinched, fully expecting to get a knife in the gut so it would truly be just the two of them.

"Boy? How would you like a ten percent cut?" Her voice suddenly grew harsh.

I said nothing. I couldn't trust this woman. Apparently, I couldn't trust the newcomer either.

Her harsh voice evaporated into sweetness as she directed it back to the stranger. "Come on, honey. It could be just like it was back in the beginning. What do you say?"

If this little cat and mouse game hadn't been so deadly serious, it would have been comical. Old people trying to talk sexy to each other, now that's funny. I found this, at that moment, to be especially true when she was not only old, but also ugly and ravaged with grenade shrapnel.

I didn't laugh, but I felt the urge to say something if only to break the tension. Also, I wanted to remind this newcomer that old Tabitha was not as loving as she was trying to make herself out to be.

"Careful, mister. She still has that knife," I said, keenly aware of how lame my words sounded, but not knowing what else to say.

"Shut up, boy!" All the bitterness in her voice instantly returned.

Apparently, I had hit on a sore spot so of course I didn't shut up. Instead, I took the proverbial screw-driver and twisted that serrated screw an extra quarter turn. "I don't think she's fooling around, mister."

I hated calling this newcomer 'mister.' I sounded like Beaver Cleaver from the old 1950s show I watched almost daily in syndication. Still, I didn't have another name to call him, so 'mister' it was.

"I said, shut up!" she shouted, and this time I wished I had.

Quick as lightning, she spun on me. The look in her one good eye verified she was nuttier than a Mr. Peanut family reunion. Her face was contorted by injuries and rage. The knife reflected the light of the single bulb dangling above us. The blade had a crimson streak on it, reminding me of my wounded thigh.

Before I could react, she came at me. For an old lady, considering her injuries, she was quick on the draw. Then again, maybe her injuries made her quicker and more dangerous, like a wounded animal in the throes of desperation.

In the midst of the commotion, one thing stood out to me. Her one good eye commanded the scene. It was so full of insanity and hate. It was a true evil eye, more so than all the eyes in the door of eyes combined.

Even if I had had time to react, what could I have done? The answer came to me in an instant: nothing. I was cornered and I had never taken any martial arts class that might have taught me how to defend against a knife attack.

I had always wanted to learn martial arts, but my parents had always said it was too expensive and too dangerous. *Thanks Mom and Dad, good call.*

She struck out with the blade. There was nothing I could do to stop it.

I screamed. I am not ashamed to admit it. I screamed like a little girl, waited for the pain, and prayed the end would be quick.

CHAPTER 39 - FAREWELLS

I remember my entire life streaming before my eyes. It didn't take long, a mere flash in the brain, like a single pulse from a strobe light. Then it was over. Birth to present, it was done.

Any second I knew the cold steel of her knife would cleave my flesh. I closed my eyes in the agony of anticipation, refusing to watch my own death. Lacking the courage to do so, I would die as the coward I was.

Absurd questions entered my mind and left as quickly. Would it hurt when the blade penetrated me? Would it slide in like a knife through warm butter or would my bones and tendons get in the way and ruff up the smoothness of the entry? And when exactly would I meet Jesus?

I assumed such trauma would sting at least a little. Then again, maybe the shock from such an injury would make it painless. I hoped for the painless route. It was an odd hope, but it was all I had at the moment, the only positive spin I could muster.

The fatal blow seemed long in coming. In fact, it seemed to be taking too long. In my impatience, I opened one eye and took a peek. My second eye followed suit just in time to watch the drama unfold.

The newcomer had reacted. He had taken Tabitha down before she reached me. He had tackled her from behind like a linebacker at the Super bowl.

I had opened my eyes just in time to see her crumple to the floor under his weight. She face-planted hard, her head connecting with the hard-packed earthen floor of the room. It was not a pleasant sound.

Now that she no longer blocked my view, I could see he was a big son of a gun. If he had tackled me, I imagined I wouldn't be getting up for a while. I hoped this was the case with old Tabitha as well.

I couldn't imagine, given her age and condition, that she would recover from that blow. Then again, this old lady had proven herself to be hard as nails and scrappy as a junkyard dog. She had survived a grenade blast, for Pete's sake! So, I wasn't sure what this latest smashup would do.

Perhaps it would do nothing. Such were my fears.

The newcomer got off of her. She remained motionless.

He was kneeling right next to me, finally allowing me to see him in detail. Yet strangely, as I think back, I don't remember noticing anything specific about him other than his overall size.

My focus, at that moment, was more on the woman. She appeared limp as a wet noodle, lying there face-down on the floor.

He placed a pair of large hands on her right shoulder and rolled her over. He was not rough, but treated her as if she were a sleeping child whom he did not want to wake up.

I'll always remember that one remaining eye of hers. It stared up at the bare bulb above. I remember seeing the bulb reflecting its image in her eye, in its vacant, unblinking stare.

Her face was frozen into a grotesque grimace. Her torn cheek dripped saliva and blood down her neck, soaking her hair and matting it to her skin. Her forehead was discoloring before our eyes where her head had hit the floor.

Despite the awfulness of her face and hair, it was the knife that demanded my attention. Unfortunately for her, she had fallen on it. Only the handle was visible. The rest was hidden deep in her gut.

I felt like puking as I stood witness to this grizzly death, but I refused myself that privilege. For one thing, I was too old to be such a pansy, or so I told myself. Secondly, I didn't want the newcomer to think I was weak. After all, I had no idea if I was next on his little killing spree. Therefore, I had to show as much machismo as possible.

"Tabitha?" the man said with the gentlest voice I had heard from him thus far.

Tabitha remained silent. Her eye remained unblinking, unmoving.

"Oh Tabitha, why did you have to go and do that?" he asked.

Tabitha stared up at him without any sign of cognizance. Clearly nobody was home. Her face was pale, pale like death with the exception of the discolored bruise and the blood.

I stared at that unblinking eye. It reminded me of the door of eyes from the tavern downtown. That door was lifeless and now so was this woman. I was about to tell the newcomer he was speaking to a dead woman —but then the dead woman interrupted.

She gasped! It was a wheezy breath and exhaled a long, low moan that lifted from somewhere deep inside.

I scampered back, nearly tripping over my own feet. I had never seen a dead person before tonight. Of course this night had been a doozy. I had seen many back up on Norfolk Avenue. Now, I saw one of them apparently come back from the grave and didn't know what to make of it.

She tried to speak, but failed. Instead a weak cough blew past her lips, splattering a mist of crimson spit particles upon her chin.

He reached down and wiped her lips dry as best as he could, but only succeeded in smearing the specks of crimson into a pink smudge. "It didn't have to end this way, Tabitha," he said with a quiver in his voice. "I never wanted it to end this way, not in a million years."

Her good eye rolled back into her skull so that only a vein-webbed yellow orb showed.

Dead now? I wondered. *Not a chance,* I realized.

She spoke. She spoke as if she were being channeled by a dark spirit. "Yes, you did," she rasped. "This is exactly how you wanted it to end!"

"I did only what I had to do," the man sobbed. "When you survived the grenades, I thought it might be a sign you could go on with your life."

She shook her head from side to side twice before lulling to the left. The pupil of her eye rolled again into view, staring and watching in a most disturbing manner.

"The treasure…." she hissed.

He shook his head. "I see now it was the foolish thinking of an old man to hope you were capable of ever changing. Even now on your deathbed, you won't let the stupid treasure go."

"It's mine!" her hissing escalated into a rage-filled noise.

That eye glared at me. I swallowed hard, again disallowing my puke from escaping.

"You stole it," he said. "How can you possibly claim it as your own?"

Talk about feeling like a third wheel. I stood there watching this strange last-rights ceremony and found myself becoming saturated with a strange sadness. Sure, I was glad that the knife meant for me had found another target. Still, I didn't want this woman to die, even if she deserved it. Up until that moment, I had always felt that some people deserved to die for the things they had done, but my point of view permanently changed then and there.

For the first time, I looked into the face of the newcomer. His face was somehow familiar and yet...not. I felt sure I had seen that face before, but where? When? The answer eluded me.

His eyes were bloodshot with anguish. Tears streamed down his aged cheeks and he sighed sighs of sadness. "I still care for you Tabitha. Regardless of everything, I still care," he muttered through the sobbing.

She whispered something, but she said it too quietly for my ears to register.

"Tabitha? Tabitha!" he said.

But Tabitha was gone.

I should have told Tabitha about Jesus, but that thought came too late. She didn't seem open to hearing it at the time. Still, I should have told her.

Sometimes you hear things your brain doesn't immediately register, but then after a moment, it deciphers the code and *voila*, recognition happens. So it was at that moment. I suddenly realized the last thing she whispered. It was a name, presumably the name of the man which stood beside me.

I looked at him and my mouth fell open, in awe. I knew now why he was so familiar and yet not. It all made sense. It all made perfect sense.

I stared at him, but his focus was elsewhere. He was staring into Tabitha's lifeless, glassed over eye. And he was crying.

CHAPTER 40 - RECOGNITIONS

Milo, I thought in disbelief. *She had said Milo.*

All three of us existed there in that spot for moments unknown, two living and one deceased. After a bit, Milo's crying subsided.

"Close your mouth," he said to me as he wiped away a straggling tear. "Do you want to look like a slack-jawed yokel?"

I hadn't realized until that moment that my mouth was open. I did as I was told, but continued to stare as if seeing a phantom from beyond the grave. It made sense now why he was so familiar.

His voice was the male version of Mrs. Scholes.' His face was also hers, albeit with a bit less age and a bit more testosterone.

I thought back to that old black and white photo that had been in Milo's Bible. The one who stood before me now was the child from the picture, much aged.

Milo looked down at the deceased gypsy and let out a sorrowful sigh. He looked so sad.

"You cared for her?" I asked.

"Right up to the very end," he answered, not taking his gaze from her corpse.

My tendency to have lack of focus suddenly kicked into overdrive. I changed the subject.

"You're dead," I said matter-of-factly.

His eyes flickered up from her body and locked with mine. They had a steely glint in them. "Are you threatening me?"

My stomach did a flip as I realized the misunderstanding. I shook my head quickly. "I mean, you're supposed to be dead."

He huffed, "Sorry to disappoint you." Then he smiled in the same manner that Mrs. Scholes always did before telling a joke. "I'm only old, not dead."

"Your mother told me you were dead."

His eyes widened and the steeliness drained away. He opened his mouth, but no words came. After what seemed to be a very long time of uncomfortable silence, he closed his mouth and looked back at Tabitha. The silence remained, but at least it was not as awkward.

I tried to bring back a feeling of normalcy to the conversation. "She's going to be so excited, I mean when she finds out you're alive and all."

Maybe it was that we were standing over a dead gypsy, but what I said didn't seem to decrease the level of weirdness. I smiled, hoping a friendly grin would help. It didn't.

"Why did she think I was…?" Again, his words seemed to stick in his throat.

"Deceased?" I said, closing his open-ended statement.

I would have used the word 'dead' or maybe even 'croaked,' but perhaps more refined language was in order given the sensitivity of the topic. But my choice of words didn't change the fact that a lifeless Tabitha was sprawled on the floor at our feet. The weirdness remained and I realized neither smiles, nor vocabulary nor anything else could improve this off-kilter situation.

Anyway, I used the word 'deceased' and he nodded. "I don't know. I guess she assumed you were dead since she hadn't seen you in about—I don't know—half a century."

"I wanted to see her, but it was too dangerous," he said, his eyes on Tabitha's body. His voice grew as he made the statement until it was nearly a shout. I took a step back in surprise.

He seemed as startled as I was and quickly lowered his voice. "It was too dangerous. Tabitha's band had too many connections. They were always watching for me. They were always watching my mother, waiting for me to show myself to her. But I was smarter than that, I stayed away for both our sakes."

I thought about that for a moment. "But now they're all dead."

He smiled a strange smile and nodded. "With them out of the picture, I doubt their organized crime connections will have any more interest in finding me."

"Why not? Wouldn't they want the treasure?" I wondered.

"Of course they would want the treasure, but I doubt anyone outside of Tabitha's family, and us of course, knows about it. Her tribe were a very secretive bunch. They wouldn't trust the syndicates they connected with." He paused, then added, "No, I'm sure you and I are now the only living people who know the location of this treasure."

"Oh," I said.

I was suddenly very aware that I was privy to a dirty little secret and the only other one who knew about it had a history of killing the others who knew. I took a cautious step away.

"Don't forget your mom. She knows about the treasure, too," I said trying to use her knowledge for my own self-preservation.

He smiled and nodded. Normally, I would have considered it a pleasant enough smile, but given my current state of mind and under the harsh glow of that single bare bulb, I couldn't tell if it was a good or an evil smile.

His grin expanded. My fears grew.

He let out a chuckle. It didn't sound particularly evil. It disturbed me nonetheless.

I flinched and went into automatic talkin'-to-Jesus mode as he slapped me on the back. I was halfway through a desperate prayer for mercy before I realized it wasn't an aggressive attack, but more how a friend would slap the back of another friend who had just told a good joke.

"I guess we should go show you to Mrs. Scholes?" I said it more like a question than a statement.

I felt his hand on my back suddenly tense up. Then it fell limp at his side. The grin left his face. I couldn't guess the reason for this sudden change in mood. "You'll be like Lazarus," I blurted out in my typical unfocused way.

"Who?"

"You know, the guy Jesus raised from the dead."

He nodded, but his face suggested he was deep in thought.

"Of course Lazarus was dead for four days and you weren't actually dead at all, so I guess it's not exactly the same. Still, I think it's about as close to a bona fide miracle as I've ever seen."

He nodded again. "Well, I guess we better go show her the miracle of me."

He didn't sound too enthusiastic. It made me wonder.

CHAPTER 41 – THROUGH THE TUNNELS

It amazed me to watch Milo shimmy out of the treasure's cave mouth and then swing like a spider monkey back into the city's drainage pipe. He moved like one fifty years his junior.

I, on the other hand, was less the spider monkey and more the sloth, slow and deliberate. Unlike the sure-climbing sloth however, I was not at home in high places.

For pride's sake, I chose to blame my wounded leg for my lack of coordination. Of course I knew deep down that my excuse was a load of hokum. Still, I needed some reason why an old man was more agile than me, if only to save my own self-esteem.

I tried to follow Milo, swinging out on the support beam. Unfortunately, I didn't gain sufficient momentum to swing back and around into the old drainage pipe. Awkwardly, I hung there like an overstuffed piñata. That's when I made a mistake. I looked down.

My heart began to race. My thoughts began to swim. My grip began to slip. This time, even my patented last knuckle, two finger on each hand grip didn't save me. I was falling!

I let out a scream, closed my eyes and waited for the coldness of the water to shock me into submission, but it never happened. I opened one eye and peeked out of my self-induced terror-coma. Milo had me by the belt and yanked me into the tunnel as if I were nothing more than a bag of wet cement.

"Thanks," I said, panting.

"Yup," he answered as casually as if he did that sort of thing all the time.

Even though we were in complete darkness in the tunnel, I felt safe with Milo. It was only a few minutes ago we were standing over the dead Tabitha and I was wondering if I was going to be next in line to meet my maker. But once somebody saves you from falling to your death, it's hard to believe they would do anything bad to you.

"Do you know the way back to the *Evil Eye?*" I asked, handing him my complete trust.

"Sure," he responded.

"Even in the dark?" I asked. I was so wishing I hadn't dropped my flashlight into the river.

"I could walk it with my eyes closed."

"That's good," I replied.

"But we're not going back to the *Evil Eye*."

This statement made me nervous. We were walking further into the darkness of the tunnel. We had no light. My guide, although I feared him less than originally, was a little off balance in my opinion, a few cards short of a complete deck, if you know what I mean. And now to top the cake with a generous blob of proverbial icing, he was leading me into unknown territory.

"Where are we going, then?" I stammered.

"We're going to the hospital. Which one is Mom at?"

"The Lutheran one," I answered.

"Good, that route is more direct."

"But this tunnel leads back to the Evil Eye."

"Not true," he answered with a chuckle. "You just missed all the branch-offs. It's easy to do as they all angle towards this main tunnel to drain into the river. Going back the other way, you'll see them."

"I doubt it. I can't see a thing in this darkness."

I heard him chuckle again.

"How do you know these tunnels so well?" I had to know.

"These tunnels have been my personal highway for fifty years. After that long, they kind of get implanted in your permanent memory."

I suddenly felt very nervous. He might have known these tunnels like the back of his hand, but I was completely out of my element. I began to think about what would become of me if I got separated from my guide. I imagined becoming like poor Gollum from *The Hobbit*. Of course, Gollum got his name from the sound that his throat made. I was more of a crybaby. I didn't want to go down in history as *Boohoo* or worse yet, *Whaaahhhh*.

Milo must have sensed my near-panic. I felt a rough, calloused hand take hold of mine.

"How long is the trip?" I asked hoping he would say it would be quick.

"Why? Do you have a hot date or something?"

"No." Obviously, Milo didn't know me very well.

"It'll take about twenty minutes, maybe a little longer with you slowing me down."

Never in my life would I have thought somebody that old would be complaining about being slowed down by the likes of someone young like me. Still, I couldn't deny my cautious feet moved slower than I suspected his could move if I weren't with him.

We traveled in silence at first, which I found unsettling. I don't know if it was my lack of focus, or if the dark tunnel and intense quiet were simply too much for me, but I craved conversation.

"I got to know something, Mr. Scholes," I said.

"Call me Milo. Mr. Scholes was my father."

"Sorry—Milo, I got to know something."

"What is it you've got to know?"

"What have you been up to for the last fifty years?"

I heard him huff, "Just trying to stay alive."

"But, you couldn't have just been living down here the whole time, hiding from the gypsies?"

"Why not?"

I didn't have an instant answer. I just didn't think that was possible. "You just couldn't have," was the best response I could muster.

I waited for his answer, but only silence responded. Again, I found the silence crushing, as if the quiet was a pillow pressed over my face, slowly smothering me into endless sleep.

Finally I could stand it no more. "Mr. Scholes?"

No answer.

"Milo?" I said. "Are you still there?" I hoped he was since I was still holding what I thought to be his hand.

"Yes," he said with a tired sigh. "I'm still here."

His voice sounded strange. Again, I recalled he was a killer of gypsies and potentially one layer short of a seven-layer salad.

This made me want to run away, but I didn't. I couldn't run from him even if I'd wanted to. The tunnels were new to me, as unfamiliar as a foreign land on an alien planet. Conversely, they were home to him. Even if I could wrench my hand free of his, I suspected I wouldn't get ten feet before he would have me in his grip, if that was his desire.

After a second longer, he continued. "I'm sorry, I guess I'm not much of a conversationalist. I've been alone for a very long time."

"It's okay," I said trying to keep from sounding nervous.

I heard him let out a deep sigh. "I just don't know where to start explaining my life."

I mustered my courage and spoke. "How about at the beginning."

He chuckled in the darkness. It was an easy-going chuckle and put my mind at ease. "I suppose the beginning is a good place to start," he said.

He began to tell, and what he told me was incredible. Still, I knew it was true. It had to be. There was simply no other explanation.

CHAPTER 42 – THE REST OF THE STORY

"How much do you already know?" he asked me.

I wasn't sure what to tell him.

"Now look here, I don't want to waste time jawing about things you already know. So tell me what you know," he added impatiently.

So, I told him everything Mrs. Scholes had told me, keeping it all in a nutshell for time's sake. When I finished, there was a pause. Then he spoke.

"Okay," I heard him say in the darkness ahead of me. "Here's what mom didn't know. Here's the rest of the story," he said, reminiscent of Paul Harvey's radio show.

*

It was 1935 and I was ripe for revenge. Those damned gypsies had just shot my dad as if he were nothing but a mangy mutt and I hated them for it.

Deep down, whether I was willing to admit it at the time or not, I was just as angry with myself as I was with them. After all, if you think about it, I was the reason my dad died. If I had listened to him and stayed away from Tabitha, he never would have been killed.

Well, the facts being as they were, he *was* killed and I knew good and well I couldn't bring him back to life. So, I decided to do what, at the time, seemed to be the next best thing. I swore to avenge his death.

That has been my job for the last fifty years. It hasn't been easy, and I can honestly say it took longer than I originally planned; but now, finally, it is done.

Retirement will be nice. To be frank, I've grown tired of doing nothing but stealing back treasure, making those gypsies miserable, and keeping mom safe without her knowing it. The same thing year after year gets a little tedious.

Perhaps because of this tiredness with my lot in life, I recently came up with a plan to end this thing once and for all. It was a good plan, if I say so myself.

I already had the grenades. I bought them on the black market shortly after the end of the Second World War. You wouldn't believe how much of that kind of stuff was available back then. Military surplus was everywhere. It was a buyer's market for sure, if you had the connections and knew where and how to buy.

I just needed to get all of Tabitha's crew together in one place so I could take care of them once and for all so I could finally be free.

My Bible was the key. The instructions there provided the means to get them all together. Tabitha's clan were a greedy breed. I knew they would all come if they thought there was a chance of getting their hands on the treasure.

So, I leaked the information to them about the Bible's alternate use as a map. Of course I did it discretely, letting them think they discovered it all on their own when in reality, it was me leaving hints and clues. I guided them like a shepherd with a flock.

Once they had the Bible, I knew it was only a matter of time before they cracked the code and congregated at the statue I had booby trapped with the grenades. I counted on their greed.

Of course things like this never go according to plan. First of all, I didn't think they'd break into Mom's and take her hostage to get the Bible. I thought I had left the clues clear enough they'd find it without resorting to such actions. Second, I didn't count on someone else beating them to the punch, but you showed up; an unexpected wild card in a deck already stacked with too many jokers.

I had no intention that anyone besides the gypsies would find my Bible or the treasure. Honestly, when you showed up, my heart sank. I certainly didn't want to blow anyone to bits who I felt didn't deserve it, especially you being such a good friend to my mom and all.

Still, I was glad it was just you. If my mother had been there, she never would have been able to get away from the blast-zone quick enough. By the way, kudos on figuring out my trap in time.

Yeah, I was watching the whole thing from one of the rooftops downtown. You had me on the edge of my seat, let me tell you. You're a smart kid.

CHAPTER 43 – UP AND OUT

Finally, we reached the end of the tunnel. This was something I was beginning to think would never happen, but that I was destined to wander the endless labyrinth under Norfolk forever with Milo as my guide. I had become so engrossed in his incredible story that, even though he continued to hold my hand, I hadn't noticed he had stopped. I bumped into him like an ignorant duckling following its mommy.

At first, I wondered if we had reached a dead end. In the dark, I couldn't see, but when I reached past Milo, I felt only a moist wall.

"Up you go," I heard his voice in the darkness.

He guided one of my hands to a cold metal rod sticking out of the wall. Then, he guided my other hand to a second rod higher up, a ladder. I climbed up, sensing Milo right behind me.

The ladder was cold against my palms and a bit slimy. I had to hold tight so as to keep from slipping. Sooner than I expected, my head bumped the ceiling. For a brief moment, light appeared before the manhole returned to its spot. I pushed against the cover. The manhole lifted and daylight flooded my light-depraved eyes. Morning had come.

The sun had not yet risen above the eastern horizon, yet after my long, dark night, this light of pre-dawn felt as bright as a noonday glare. I squinted and looked around. As my eyes adjusted to the brightness, I recognized my location. I was emerging into the far end of the Lutheran Hospital parking lot.

"Why don't you take a picture. It'll last longer," I heard Milo's voice echo up from under me.

I wiggled out like a worm escaping saturated soil. Milo emerged behind me.

I looked at him for the first time in good natural light and grinned. He was nothing more or less than an old man, a bit grimy but otherwise ordinary.

It seemed funny as I looked at him then, to think I had ever been afraid of him. Of course, lurking in a dark tunnel, one's perspective can be far different than sitting on parking lot asphalt in the light of a new day.

Even his voice sounded ordinary, no longer eerie or foreboding, but normal. I still knew his unusual history, but somehow now as I looked at him, I no longer had any fear he was anything other than my best friend's son.

"What's with the stupid grin?"

I hadn't realized I'd been grinning stupidly or otherwise until he mentioned it. *Yup*, I thought. *He's just a gruff old run-of-the-mill Norfolkian geezer.* I thought more on that and determined he was a lot like his mother.

I didn't stop grinning and after a moment, he simply shook his head and started to replace the manhole cover. I jumped into action to help. Now that I saw him for what he was, just an old man, my upbringing suggested I assist him in such tasks; respect for elders and all that jazz.

I looked around cautiously, afraid somebody had witnessed our strange entrance into the realm above, but as far as I could tell, no one saw. The morning was young. The parking lot was mostly empty and we had emerged into the lot's furthest corner. This was right beside the drainage ditch which had been built to keep the lot from flooding. The few cars that were parked there were unoccupied and likely belonged to people who had spent the night there either as patients, overnight visitors, or employees.

With the manhole cover back in place, it was time to begin the next task. I took maybe ten paces towards the hospital entrance before noticing that Milo was not following.

I looked back. He was just standing there beside the manhole as if he found safety in being near the entrance to his creepy secret lair. A stone-cold expression had conquered his face.

"Are you alright?" I asked.

He nodded slowly.

He didn't look alright. He looked positively ill and I desperately hoped I was not going to have to witness another classic Scholes heart attack episode.

"Are you ready to go in?" I said, antsy to get this show on the road.

He didn't answer.

Suddenly, the man I had first perceived as a threat, and then as a senior citizen, now looked like a helpless child. I wondered how many other layers were hidden in this human onion.

"Milo?"

No answer.

"Mr. Scholes?" I knew he didn't like the formal title, but I was kind of at a dead end as to how to get him to respond.

"I can't do it," he muttered.

"You can't do what?" I was thoroughly confused.

"I'm not ready to see her."

Maybe it was because I had never personally experienced these sorts of life events, but I had great difficulty understanding the dilemma. "You've wanted to see your mom for fifty years."

He said nothing, but nodded.

"And now you want to wait some more?"

"I don't know what I want, kid," he answered with a tired shrug.

I just stared at this man who was both old and young at the same time. I didn't know how to fix this for him. I just wanted it fixed. I just wanted the adventure to end.

"I don't want to wait, but what if…." he stopped mid-sentence, as if the words had all jammed up in his throat.

The boy persona was now shining out so much from him that I had a hard time seeing the old man within. He was so vulnerable, so helpless. This was the kid from the old black and white photo.

"What if she won't want to see me?"

"That's ridiculous," I said with far less sensitivity than I probably should have shown at that moment.

"What if by staying away too long, I hurt her too much?"

"Milo, you're her son. She loves you. Of course she'll want to see you. For Pete's sake, she thinks you're dead. My only fear is that the truth will shock her into a coma."

"That's not funny."

"Sorry," I said and I meant it. My patience was just wearing a little thin.

"Dad wouldn't have died if it weren't for me," he sobbed as he wiped tears from his leathery cheeks.

As the sun crept over the horizon, the light shone on me both physically and figuratively. Now I understood his problem.

I came over to him and put my hand on his as if he were actually the child I now perceived him to be. "I'm telling you Milo, she won't see things that way. She blames Tabitha and her band. She never blamed you, not for a moment."

He nodded and took my hand. I felt he didn't believe me totally, but hopefully he trusted me.

"How will I know if that's the truth," he mumbled.

I shrugged. "There's only one way to find out."

He looked so frightened. I tried to recall how I had perceived him so recently—a tough as nails fighter and victor of the great Fifty Year Gypsy

War. Now all I could see was a little boy who had hidden inside the skin of an old man, but was doing so no longer. This was the boy who just wanted to be loved by his mother.

"Come on," I guided him along towards the hospital entrance. Together, we entered.

CHAPTER 44 – HESITATIONS AND RESERVATIONS

To this day, I thank God I was in Norfolk, Nebraska and not some larger, more metro-sized sort of place. If the town had been larger like Chicago, or even Omaha, there would have been a lot more red tape.

Even as it was, it was not easy just waltzing into a hospital one day after an imposter nurse tried to commit murder, not to mention all the other things that had occurred in the town throughout the previous night. I never found out if the morgue was located in the hospital, but if it was, I was sure it was packed to the gills with mangled bodies.

The police and the press were everywhere. Both groups had a million and one questions for me and Milo. They virtually engulfed us the moment we entered the hospital.

The reporters made me nervous as they came at me like a swarm of hungry mosquitoes. I didn't want to be photographed or put on TV. Perhaps if the story had been a happier one, I wouldn't have minded. This however was nothing but a tragedy, a very sad tragedy.

As nervous as the reporters made me, it was nothing compared to how the cops made me feel. The instant I popped up on their radar, they came running. I found myself not knowing what to do or how to respond. I had suspicions I was about to be, once again thrown to the ground and cuffed like a criminal.

They rushed me, but thankfully I remained cuff-free. It turned out Mrs. Scholes had filled them in on what was more or less going on.

So, sufficiently vindicated by what Mrs. Scholes had told them about me, the police first of all dismissed the press. I was thankful for that. I didn't want to be bombarded with paparazzi questions.

Unfortunately, once the reporters left, the cops started their own bombardment. I squirmed under the pressure of their questioning. They had an interrogatory vibe to them, but at least my wrists didn't get sore as they would have with cuffs. I suppose that was a plus.

As I felt I had no real choice in the matter, I answered their questions for the most part, conveniently forgetting the detail that Milo was responsible for the explosion and the resulting deaths. I did tell them about the body they would find in the treasure cave. I knew I would probably have to take the stand on Milo's behalf in order to convince the court he had killed her in my defense, but honestly that wasn't at the top of my priority list in terms of my concerns at that particular moment.

I suspected there would be a thorough investigation at some point in the future. Again, I was thankful this was a small town with limited investigatory resources.

After satisfying the police, we were given the standard 'don't leave town' line and then given the all clear to go see Mrs. Scholes. They had relayed to me how worried she had been. They'd mentioned nothing about what she felt about Milo, then again she had no idea yet that he was still alive. I honestly hoped the shock of this new development wouldn't give her another heart attack.

I guided her prodigal son by the arm as if he were my ill-fitted prom date. It still surprised me how much he had changed in such a short time. His transformation from tough old rounder to timid little boy was quite the shock.

It seemed odd to me that this tough old fighter now seemed overcome with the fear he might be in trouble with his mommy. It seemed ridiculous, yet it was the reality.

"Wait," he said with a whisper.

We were halfway down the hall to Mrs. Scholes' room. I stopped and looked at him.

His face had taken on a sickly grey tinge and I suspected this was not just because he'd spent most of his time away from the sun, down in the Norfolk City storm drainage system.

"I just can't do this." His voice sounded so weak, so resigned.

Well, a boy's patience can only be stretched so far. I had been through a lot. I felt drained physically, mentally, and spiritually. I just didn't have anything left to give in the way of comfort and coaxing at that moment.

I tried to pull him along, but he was a stubborn mule, planting his feet and standing his ground. Again, he reminded me of his mother who, as I recalled, had once planted herself to the ground in front of an approaching tornado.

"We've been through all of this," I said with exasperation. "She doesn't blame you for your father's death."

"But she doesn't even know I'm alive. How do you think she'll take this news?"

I shrugged and continued to yank at his arm, but it was a fight I lacked both the strength to win and the motivation to continue. Eventually, I let go of him and surrendered to the inevitable stale-mate.

"What if she changes her attitude once she sees me?"

The heck with surrender, I thought as I rallied my second-wind strength and began once again to pull at him.

"What if everything she told you was based on thinking I was dead?"

I stopped tugging again as the last gust of my second wind blew away and disappeared.

"Why don't you go in first," he said after a brief pause.

"What good will that do?" I responded.

"Feel her out. See what she really thinks about me. See if I should go in or not."

I nodded. All in all, this wasn't a bad plan. In actuality, it wouldn't have mattered to me at that point if it had been a completely stupid plan, as long as it got him moving in the right direction.

I took his arm again, but now I was too exhausted to pull. This time he came with me down the hall until we stood just outside her door.

I had no doubt Mrs. Scholes held no grudge against her son regardless of whether he was dead or alive. Still, she assumed he was dead and I *was* concerned about the shock factor of her finding out he was still among the living.

I most certainly didn't want to send poor old Mrs. Scholes to an early grave. So, just as one does not simply jump into a recently thawed lake, so too, I would help my neighbor slowly wade into the truth she was about to discover.

I looked at Milo. He had the same look I had once, when I was younger and had been caught by my parents stealing desert before dinner.

I smiled at him. It was meant to be a reassuring smile, but he remained stone-faced.

I put my hand on the door knob and began to turn, but before I could open it, Milo's hand grabbed mine. I looked at him. Fresh tears ran down his weathered cheeks.

"What now?" God knows I was trying with all that was in me to be patient, but my patience had grown paper-thin with lack of sleep and exhaustion from my nocturnal adventure.

"We need some sort of a signal," he said.

"No, we don't."

"Yes, we do," he responded, lobbing the proverbial tennis ball back to my side of the court.

I rolled my eyes and let out a moan. I was so tired, so completely exhausted.

"Listen, if Mom sounds like she wants to see me then open the door and let me in. But if she doesn't want to see me..."

"For the hundredth time, she *will* want to see you!" I interrupted.

"Let me finish." His hand was still on mine. It was shaking and I remembered he was more than just a little boy who was about to see his mother. He was a little boy in an old man's body who was about to see his mother for the first time in half a century.

He continued. "If she doesn't want to see me, then open the door just a crack and say you're going to get coffee from the cafeteria."

"What? I don't drink coffee."

"Fine," he said dryly. "What do you drink?"

I thought for a moment. "Coke."

"Fine. Say you're going to the cafeteria to get a coke."

"Why would I want a coke?"

"You won't! It's just a signal!"

I sighed. In my mind, the whole needing a signal thing was one hundred percent irrelevant. I knew Mrs. Scholes better than he did. I knew she would want to see her long lost son, but just to get past the whole issue, I nodded.

"If you say that, I'll make like a tree and leave. And I don't want you to tell her anything about me, *capisce*?"

"*Capisce*? What does *capisce* mean?"

"It means you understand."

I nodded. Under other circumstances, I might have laughed at the irony of not understanding that *capisce* meant understand, but these weren't other circumstances and given my exhaustion, the act of laughing seemed too difficult.

I didn't laugh. I didn't even smile. Instead, I opened the door.

"Mrs. Scholes?" I said as I entered.

She didn't respond.

CHAPTER 45 – THE POWER OF PRAYER

A chill crawled out of some dark hiding place deep within me. It ran up my spine like a frightened squirrel up a tree as I quickly closed the door behind me.

"Mrs. Scholes?" I said again.

Still no response.

I ran over to her bedside. She was nothing more than a lifeless lump under a bed sheet.

Panic enveloped me as I remembered all the movies I had seen over the course of my life. In those movies, whenever a hospital patient passed away, they always pulled the sheet up over the deceased person's body, creating a death shroud.

All memories of my exhausted state instantly evaporated. In its place was a renewed energy, but not the good kind. I could feel my heart beating, pumping like a piston under the hood of a dragster from Hell.

I pulled down the death shroud, fearful of the blank stare I was sure would meet me. Despite the fear, I fought the urge to close my eyes. I was determined to look into her face one final time.

I let out a moan as I looked. The cadaver that stared up at me was less hideous than I had feared. It took a moment for my mind to register that it was not a dead body at all and definitely not Mrs. Scholes. It was nothing but her pillow.

I heard the flush of a toilet and a sink's faucet running. I turned to her bathroom as the door opened and I beheld a sight I will never forget. It was the unbelievably resurrected Mrs. Scholes.

To my mind, this was nothing short of a miracle. The bathroom was a tomb, its door the entrance from one side of eternity to the other. I actually thought I heard a heavenly choir sing as she walked out into the world of the living.

Well, I can tell you I gave her the biggest hug I ever dealt out to anyone in my entire life and that included the time I hugged my mom the day she said I no longer had to wear bolo ties to school. I feared I might squeeze her too hard, in her fragile condition, but I couldn't help myself.

The surprising thing was, she hugged me back just as fiercely. "I am so glad to see you! I was so worried!" she said.

I released her from the hug and took a step back so she could get around me and back to her bed. She smiled, but tears streaked down her face.

"Don't cry Mrs. Scholes." I didn't like to see her so sad.

She wiped her face dry with the back of her hand. She said nothing, but her expression spoke volumes.

I was trying so hard to act macho. I didn't want her to know I had written her off as dead just moments ago.

"Are you okay?" she asked. "You look pale, like you've just seen a ghost."

That was a bit too close to the truth. "It's just lack of sleep," I lied.

I had a feeling she saw through my ruse. In evidence of this, a fresh set of tears appeared in the corners of her eyes and began their trip down her heavily lined cheeks.

Without either of us saying another word, we hugged again. This time, the hug took longer than before.

"Did you find what you were looking for?" she asked.

Again, I pulled back. I wasn't sure what to say. Sure, I found the treasure, but I also found so much more. For the life of me, I wasn't sure how to bring up the topic of Milo. I ended up doing nothing but staring down at my feet.

She shuffled by me and sat down on the end of her bed. "The doctors say I'm doing much better, but if you want me to sit down to take your news, then fine."

I sat down beside her, not knowing where to begin. "I found the treasure," I blurted out.

She smiled. "You did much more than find treasure."

Her smile was odd and made me wonder what she meant by that. It was a puzzlement. I couldn't figure out how in the world she would know anything about the man I found with the treasure who now stood just outside waiting to enter.

"There's something you're not telling me," she continued.

A lump caught in my throat. *How did she know? How could she possibly know?*

"The police told me about the explosion."

"Oh, that," I said with relief.

"Of course that. What did you think I was talking about?"

I ignored that last question. "All the gypsies are dead."

Her smile disappeared. "That's sad."

"I thought you hated the gypsies?"

She nodded "I hate what Tabitha's family did, long ago. But they were still people."

We sat awhile in silence, letting that statement sink in. I had so much more to tell her, but I was having trouble forming the words. I was sure if a pin dropped just then, it would have landed with a sound equivalent to a sonic boom. Then Mrs. Scholes dropped that pin.

"I've been praying," she said, shattering the profound silence.

I looked up at her in shock. That was probably the last thing I had expected her to say, given her aversion to God.

"When did you start praying?" I asked.

"I started last night." She laughed a mirthless laugh. "I haven't done that for a very long time." She scrunched her eyebrows into thinking mode. "Probably not since Milo left."

"Oh," was all I could manage as a response. It was a strange coincidence that she stopped praying when Milo left, and began again unbeknownst to her, when he was about to return.

"But ever since last night—well, I started praying for you to come out of this safe and sound, and you know what?"

I shrugged my response.

"Every time I closed my eyes and bowed my head, an image of Milo entered my mind."

My eyes grew wide. I trusted in God and believed in miracles, but this was a lot to swallow in one gulp.

"But he wasn't the young man I remembered. In my mind, I saw him as he might look today." She laughed again. "I guess that was my mind's image of your guardian angel."

I didn't say anything. What could I possibly have said?

It was true after all. Milo *had* been my guardian angel, no doubt about that. He had saved me from the enemy and brought be out of their clutches all safe and sound.

But he was not just my angel, I was willing to bet he had been an angel to both of us. I suspected he had saved us from tornadoes and rabid dogs. Furthermore, I bet dollars to donuts he was the one who had pulled Mrs. Scholes from the burning wreckage of her car all those years ago.

She slapped my knee with her hand. "There must be something to this prayer stuff, because here you are, safe and sound."

We sat there, allowing the silence to once again take over. I was exhausted. My brain was as worn out as my muscles. Still, I knew the truth when I heard it. There was definitely power in prayer, no question.

"I think I believe in God now," she said, breaking the silence once again.

What a bomb to drop on me. And that was coming from somebody who recently literally had bombs dropped on them.

She smiled. "There is a God," she said and then paused. "That's a statement that takes your breath away, doesn't it?"

In retrospect, the dumbfounded stare I gave her then probably was not the best response. Regardless, it was how I responded.

"I see now that my bitterness towards Jesus was all a result of losing my family fifty years ago. Now I see how harboring such bitterness is nothing but wasted energy."

"It's not easy to let go of bitterness," I said, not of my own wisdom, but something that someone wiser than me had once said, probably either my dad, mom, or my pastor.

She nodded. "No, I suppose it isn't. But it's refreshing when you finally do let it go. I tell you, I feel free for the first time in a very long time."

I put my arm around her and she leaned into me. I could feel her body vibrate with repressed sobs.

"You're all I have left," she murmured.

That statement reminded me of the man waiting in the hall. She had so much more than she realized. Stupidly, I had forgotten about him. I hoped to God he was still out there, waiting.

CHAPTER 46 - HOMECOMING

I sat there on the bed with old Mrs. Scholes and considered just letting my exhaustion take over. I was no guru of focus even on a good day, and this was far from a good day. My brain wanted nothing more than to shut down and recharge.

Unfortunately, this was not an option, not yet anyway, not until my job was done. I thought about all I had already accomplished in the last twenty-four hours. I had cheated death not once by the thugs who broke into my neighbor's house, not twice at the old farmhouse ruins, not thrice at the hands of an impostor nurse, not four times at the grenade pile inside the ancient landmark, but five times when old Tabitha cornered my sorry butt in the treasure cave.

Despite everything I had overcome, I could not, for the life of me, figure out how to let my best friend in on the little secret about her son. Trying to figure the escape from this dilemma only resulted in further fatigue.

"What's eating at you?" she asked, breaking my concentration.

I looked at her. She was staring at me with concern on her face.

"Nothing," I fibbed.

She let out a huff. "Boy, we've been friends way too long for me to accept lies from you. Now spill it."

I tried to look at her, but she kept going all blurry. I wiped away my tears so as to see her clearly, but she remained clear only momentarily. After all I had been through, I would have thought my machismo would have kicked in. Apparently, I was wrong.

"What is it?" she pushed me to divulge.

"I was just thinking about your son." There, that was a good start, and an honest start too.

"Milo?"

I nodded.

"Oh, don't worry about him. He had faith in God. I know he's in a better place."

Although I was glad Mrs. Scholes was growing spiritually, for the moment, it only hindered me. I would have to somehow tell her Milo was not in that great of a place after all. In fact, he was waiting just outside in the hallway. I let out a sigh, majorly bummed that things were not progressing as I had hoped.

"Holy cow kid, I can't help you if you're not straight with me." Her voice strained with hints of impatience.

I put my head in my hands and rubbed my temples with the tips of my fingers. Some man I was, sobbing and blubbering on. I guess I still had some growing to do.

I heard the room's door open. I heard a familiar voice. "You're not very good at this are you?"

I looked up. Milo must have been listening from the other side of the door. He entered the room, and not a moment too soon. It was true, I was not very good at this. I needed help.

I looked from Milo to Mrs. Scholes and back again. Her expression was strange. His mirrored hers, evidence they shared much of the same DNA.

I looked back at Mrs. Scholes. A glimmer lit up her eyes. Her lip quivered slightly.

"Do I know you?" she stammered.

He stood there trying to form words, but nothing came from his open mouth.

"You look familiar," she added.

He said nothing, but entered the room further. He walked up to his mother not as a man, but with the unsure steps of a child who didn't know if he was in trouble or not.

At her age, Mrs. Scholes eyes weren't what they once were. This was something she had told me on numerous occasions and more often in recent years. Now as he drew nearer, her peepers widened.

He reached out his hands as if he wanted to hold hers. He hesitated in mid-reach.

This scene stalled, like a photograph stuck in time. The glitch was momentary however as she suddenly reached out, taking his hands in hers.

"Am I dreaming?" she gasped. Her eyes were now as wide as saucers.

Milo still said nothing, but shook his head.

"Have I died?" she inquired.

"No," I said to her.

The silence that followed was awkward for me. I suspected it was not as much so for them. I was kind of the third wheel at this little family reunion and quite frankly, didn't know what to do with myself.

"I've come home?" He said this not with conviction but as if asking permission.

I began to feel lightheaded and the room started to spin. It was as if the world was suddenly rotating on its axis much quicker than normal.

At first, this feeling confused me, but then I realized the culprit. I had been holding my breath much as one does when watching a particularly exciting scene in a movie. I exhaled and inhaled a few times and the lightheadedness gradually went away.

Mrs. Scholes let go of his hands and looked at me. Fresh tears were forming in her eyes.

"It's okay," I said to her. I used the most encouraging voice I could muster.

"It just can't be." Her voice was shaky. Her expression was odd.

I said nothing. Neither did Milo. What could either of us have said at that point anyway? So, we just stood there and let this deluge of unbelievable information bombard her brain.

I squinted my eyes shut and then reopened them. I looked at her. She seemed to have aged another ten years then and there. I worried that if I shut my eyes again, she would be nothing but a dusty pile of bones. I refused therefore to do so much as even blink.

I looked closely into her eyes and despite her rapid aging, I believe I saw a spark flickering to life within her. I prayed it was a good spark, related to her being young at heart.

She reached out with one of her hands and took his again. With the other, she took one of mine. "Well, it is a fact. God almighty does answer prayers and I have the proof right here in front of me," she said and then broke down, wailing.

I looked at Milo. He looked back at me. I can tell you I was at a loss of what to do at that moment and I believe he was as well. So, we just held her hands until the crying subsided.

Finally, she regained composure and looked up at us. Tears were still falling, but at least things had calmed a bit.

Despite her tears, I saw a smile form upon her lips. "Well, I think I'm ready to go back to church this Sunday," she said through a lingering sob.

"Me, too," Milo said with a whisper.

I agreed, "Me, too."

CHAPTER 47 – AN UNEXPECTED VISIT

Many years after the end of the great Gypsy War, after the passing of Mrs. Scholes; in fact the day of Milo's funeral, I received an unexpected visit.

The visit occurred at Milo's burial. I was watching his casket as it slowly descended into the vault. The lowering device was quite intriguing to me. A man used a crank to lower the casket.

In my mind's eye, I saw through the lid and could see Milo's body and the Bible that rested upon his chest. Of course, this was not *The Bible*. That one had been blown to smithereens by the grenades. The one that now lowered with Milo's body into the earth however was just as special. For it was this Bible which Milo had read in both his personal devotions as well as to his mother. Mrs. Scholes' eyesight had continued to deteriorate and for the last years of her life, Milo read the scriptures to her every day.

As the crank continued to turn and the casket continued to descend, I looked to the adjacent grave. There lay Mrs. Scholes.

Tears came to my eyes as I thought back to that day of reunion in the hospital. I believe such memories will entice tears for the rest of my days.

From my old neighbor's grave, I looked up. The Nebraska sun was hot that day and the few who had gathered for the ceremony were shiny with sweat. In the distance was a large cottonwood. Under that tree, cooling in the shade, stood a man and a woman.

They drew my attention because they weren't dressed formally as one going to a funeral might dress. I would have thought they were simply there to visit the grave of some loved one, except they seemed focused on Milo's ceremony.

The coffin reached the bottom and loose dirt began to cover Milo's earthly remains. I tried to keep my focus on the burial, but even as an adult, my attention was short.

I found myself glancing back at that old cottonwood. Every time I looked, they were there, the staring duo. They were now sitting, their backs against the trunk of the tree; watching and waiting. From that distance, I could identify no details of these strangers other than the flowing dress of the woman which sprawled out upon the ground like colorful liquid wax as she sat against the trunk.

I had no idea what attracted their stares. Certainly it wasn't the size of Milo's burial ceremony. Not many were in attendance.

Milo, having lived in seclusion up until the end of the great Gypsy War, had trouble adjusting and had remained somewhat reclusive until the day of his death. For that reason, I felt privileged that he considered me his friend and confidant.

One by one, the few attendees paid their final respects and left the scene until I was the lone remainder. I looked once more to the distant cottonwood, but the sun had changed position and shone directly into my eyes.

Squinting against that late-day glare, I made out the silhouette of that mighty tree, but the lurkers who had been under it had vanished. After all I had been through, I had become prone to fits of occasional paranoia and feelings of being watched. Now, with the lurkers departed, I conjectured that at least today, the paranoia had been unfounded. They had been nothing more than common cemetery visitors.

With the others gone and the grave filled in, I said my own piece. "Well, Milo and Mrs. Scholes. I know neither of you were much for this sentimental crud, but I guess now you have no choice but to listen to me. I was never too good at making friends, but you were both mine. I was never too good at school, but you made me feel I had worth. I don't know if I ever told you how much you two meant to me, so I am telling you now. You two meant the world."

I stood there as the sun began to slide behind the horizon, stretching and deepening the shadows. Finally, I wrapped it up. "Well, I guess I'll see you both again someday. Until then, you two take care."

The sun had now disappeared. In the twilight, I stared at the two graves before me. I knew this was an end to a chapter in my life. Still, I felt a sense of contentment, the sort that comes only from God showing his presence. I closed my eyes and prayed, expressing my thanks for giving me these two unique individuals and allowing them to be a part of my life.

The last remnants of daylight were dying. As I turned to leave, realization struck. I wasn't alone!

I came face to face with the cottonwood lurkers. Neither of them spoke. They didn't need to. I knew who they were.

"Only gypsies have ever been able to sneak up on me like that," I said, trying to keep a courageous tone in my voice.

One of them nodded in response. He was middle-aged, but I could see few other features in the dusk.

I paused, not knowing how to tactfully ask my next question. "I thought you were all...."

"Dead?" the woman interrupted. The low light camouflaged her appearance, but her voice expressed beauty.

The word she had uttered had bite, germinating a lump of fear within me.

"Well, we didn't all die that day," she said. "A few survived the blast and a few more weren't even there. I, for example, had been told to stay behind and man the camp. That night the survivors trickled into camp. We did what we could for them, to ease their suffering. Many died that night and the next day. We buried them in the woods, unmarked but never forgotten."

"I'm sorry it all happened," I said truthfully.

The man piped in. "But it did happen."

I said nothing. The lump of fear expanded exponentially. I took a step back, preparing to flee.

"We understand why you did what you did," he continued. "We would have done the same in your shoes."

I wondered if they knew how little of a role I played in the whole ambush event. I wondered if they knew the true mastermind of the explosion was lying behind me under six feet of earth.

"Actually, you did us a favor," the woman blurted out.

I blinked, trying to understand, but failing.

"Tabitha was gypsy royalty. Her family had ruled our group for generations. Her word was always final. We did her bidding without question. But after her death, our eyes were opened to the extent of our brainwashing.

"Once she was dead, we became free to think for ourselves. And we realized we could be so much more than we were. We could lead honest lives. We could choose a life outside of crime.

"Sure we were gypsies and always would be. But the definition of what that meant changed for us. We aren't ashamed of our past. We aren't afraid of our future. We simply want to live.

The man spoke now. "Tabitha's death gave us new life. We wanted you to know."

With that said, they walked past me and stopped before Milo's grave. Then they knelt upon the freshly-turned dirt.

"God bless you Milo Scholes," one of them said.

"Yes, God bless you and your dear mother," the other chimed in.

I looked at these two as new tears clouded my eyes. An owl hooted from the cottonwood. I looked just as it took off, barely visible against the backdrop of night.

And when I looked back, the gypsies were gone.

THE END

A NOTE FROM THE AUTHOR

I really did grow up at 405 South First Street in Norfolk Nebraska. My father spoke once to an elderly someone who claimed to have lived in the house years ago when they were children. That person recalled memories of being rushed into the attic to hide from gypsies. It was believed that this group, if given the opportunity, would abduct children from their homes. This was the origins of my book.

Many of the places I describe in this story existed during the time the story takes place. Examples of this include *Memorial Field* and *Bob Zestos*. Also, the *Benson Bunnies* was, and still is a real team and they are far tougher than what their name suggests.

On the other side of the coin, my parents never forced me to wear bolo ties, although I may have worn them once or twice of my own volition as a bold fashion statement. Also, to my knowledge, there has never been a real place called *The Evil Eye* and the same goes for the statue I describe standing in front of it.

In summary, I want to be clear that this is a work of fiction based on a real location. I am still fond of Norfolk and consider it to be my hometown. In that regard, I want to be clear any negative connotations concerning it was written strictly for the reader's entertainment and not meant to be taken as an insult to the town, its citizens, the competency of its police force, gypsies as a group, etc.

Sincerely,
Shawn D. Brink

PS: Go Panthers!

ABOUT THE AUTHOR

Shawn D. Brink was born in Clovis New Mexico, but has lived in eastern Nebraska since he was five. He holds an undergraduate degree in Secondary Education from Wayne State College and a graduate degree in Management from Bellevue University. His interests (Besides writing) include church, playing guitar, and spending time with his wife and four children.

It was during his time as a student at Wayne that he attempted his first novel. That manuscript was never published, but it infected Shawn with an incurable writing virus. Shawn has since had many stories featured in various publications. *Hell on Earth* is his fourth published novel and completes *The Space Between* trilogy.

Keep up to date with Shawn at

http://gabrielshornpress.com/shawnbrink

https://shawnbrinkauthor.wordpress.com/

https://www.facebook.com/shawnbrinkauthor1

https://twitter.com/shawnbrinkauth2

www.ingramcontent.com/pod-product-compliance
Lightning Source LLC
Chambersburg PA
CBHW051508170626
46811CB00002B/712